THE LOST GARDEN

A note on the author

Helen Humphreys is the author of the novels *Leaving Earth* and *Afterimage* and four books of poetry. She lives in Kingston, Ontario.

THE LOST GARDEN

Helen Humphreys

BLOOMSBURY

For Madeleine

First published in Great Britain 2003
This paperback edition published 2004

Bloomsbury Publishing Plc, 38 Soho Square, London W1D 3HB

A CIP catalogue record for this book is
available from the British Library

ISBN 0 7475 6813 8

10 9 8 7 6 5 4 3 2 1

All papers used by Bloomsbury Publishing are natural, recyclable
products made from wood grown in well-managed forests.
The manufacturing processes conform to the
environmental regulations of the country of origin.

Printed in Great Britain by Clays Ltd, St Ives plc

www.bloomsbury.com/helenhumphreys

Say this when you return,
"I came by the wrong road,
And saw the starved woods burn."

RICHARD CHURCH

Nothing will catch you.
Nothing will let you go.
We call it blossoming—
the spirit breaks from you and you remain.

JORIE GRAHAM

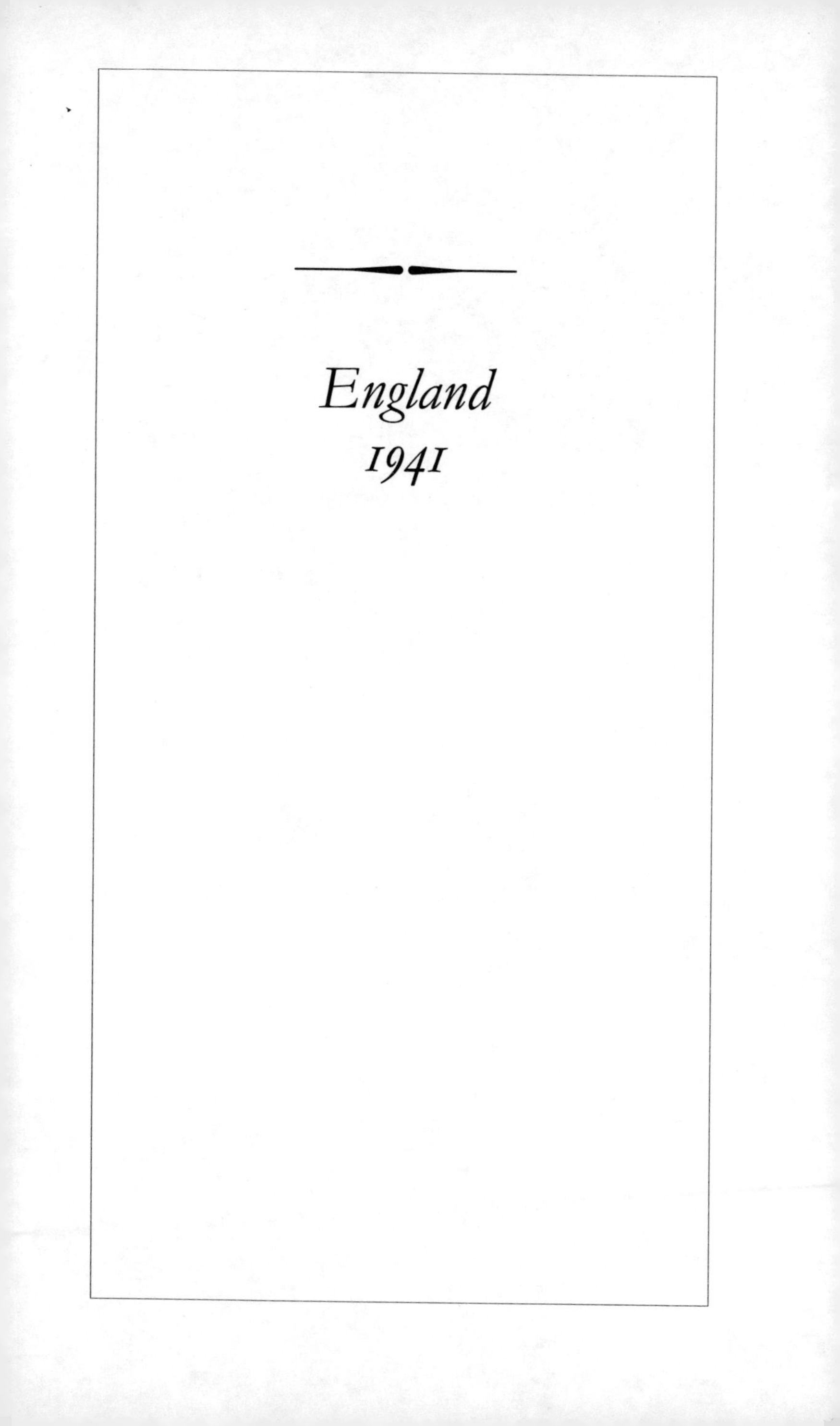

England
1941

We step out into lamplight and evening opening around us. This felt moment. Our brief selves. Stars a white lace above the courtyard.

We walk the streets of London. It is seven years ago. We didn't meet, but we are together. This is real. This is a book, dusty from the top shelf of a library in Mayfair. The drowned sound of life under all that ink, restless waves breaking on this reading shore. Where I wait for you. I do. In a moment. In a word. Here on the street corner. Here on this page.

But it is shutting all around me, even now, this moment that I stopped. The story disappears as I speak it. Each word a small flame I have lit for you, above this darkened street.

I

What can I say about love? You might see me sitting in this taxi, bound for Paddington Station—a thirty-five-year-old woman with plain features—and you would think that I could not know anything of love. But I am leaving London because of love.

I wasn't born in the city, have only lived here for the past ten years, since I left gardening college and came to work at the Royal Horticultural Society. But what is love if not instant recognition? A moment of being truly equal to something. What I recognized in this place, from the moment I arrived here, was something within myself that I didn't even know was there. Something under the skin, in the blood. A pulse of familiarity. The wild, lovely clutter of London. Small streets that twisted like rivers. Austere stone cathedrals. The fast, muddy muscle of the Thames, holding the city apart from itself; the tension of that moving gap, palpable, felt. I have leaned over the stone balustrade of the Embankment in the dark, the true dark now of the blackouts when even starlight is an act of treachery. In blacked-out London, people, once familiar with the city, bump along the streets, fumbling from building to building as though blind. But I have stood beside the Thames and felt it there, twining beneath my feet like a root.

But this is what can no longer be trusted. Every day the landscape is radically altered. Houses become holes. Solids become spaces. Anything can disappear overnight. How can love survive this fact?

The streets are almost empty. I look up as we drive along the Vauxhall Bridge Road and from between two buildings I see a flicker of green that leads to Vincent Square and the stone face of the Royal Horticultural Society looking down into the Westminster Play Ground. Only yesterday I was there in my life, hurrying back from lunch with Roy Peake. At the corner of the square a Canadian soldier said goodbye to his girl. "So long, sweetheart." I liked the jaunty ring of it. I had been walking up the steps of the Royal Horticultural Society, listening to Roy Peake prattle on about his "unknown pear." I think he is secretly hoping he won't be able to identify it so he can name it after himself. *Peake's Pear*. I have to admit it does sound right. Certain. The stumble of *p*'s like two perfect, companionable, musical notes.

Peake's Pear. I was thinking this, treading the grey stone steps back to my office, when the voice called from along the square with such confidence I turned right around. I am always envious of confidence. This is why I was first drawn to Roy Peake. He spoke so passionately one day about old local apples, standing in my office doorway, holding an 'Orange Goff' in one hand and a 'Pigeon's Heart' in the other. This was back when his interests were more varied, before the eternal days of the "unknown pear."

Can words go straight to the heart? Is this possible? Can words be as direct as the scent of roses? A man calls from a street corner and I turn my head to the voice as I would turn to the fragrance of a climbing rose, tangled through an arbour.

I have said my farewells to my fellow boarders at Mrs. Royce's house on Denbigh Street. I have said my farewells and felt nothing. In the two years I lived there I did not befriend any of them, and even though Mr. Gregory tried to make me like him, I never did. Besides those I worked with, I have no one else to say goodbye to; but now, as I drive away from where I've lived, I feel unbearably sad. There is the street where a magnificent cherry tree grows. I will miss it flowering this year. I will likely never see it again.

I look through the taxi window, unable to not watch the familiar streets reel away from me. The wind sways the barrage balloons tethered above the buildings, and they lean the same way, like boats swinging with the tide, at anchor in the harbour.

Most of the buildings themselves are padded with sandbags around the base. Windows are criss-crossed with strips of gummed paper—a pathetic attempt to keep the glass intact when the blasts hit. But there are more windows gone than not. I have walked by restaurants and public houses, their windows shattered into the street and the patrons eating dinner or standing up at the bar with a pint, as though this is a perfectly ordinary occurrence, as though there have never been windows in this, their local establishment.

There are Air Raid Shelter placards on most shop windows and buildings. There are queues of children outside the underground stations in the mornings, waiting to secure a space for that evening's shelter.

I know how to judge the relative distance of an exploding bomb. Those far enough away not to inflict any personal damage make a dull, crumpled sound, like that from a collision between an automobile and a lamppost. The bombs the Germans drop that are close enough to kill emit a strangled whistle, not unlike that of a sort of huge, maniacal teakettle.

I cannot reconcile myself to these changes. I cannot continue adapting to the destruction of the city. London is burning now. In January, eight of the city churches and the Guildhall were destroyed by fire. I could see the smoke from my boarding-house bedroom, swaying against the night sky. I could see the red blossoms of fire blooming along the rooftops.

The taxi winds its way towards the station. Past a row of terraced houses, one suddenly gone out of the middle. Children already clambering over the pile of bricks someone's home has become. An accordion of staircase poking out of the top of the rubble. A flag of torn curtain fluttering from under a window frame. A looking-glass hanging crookedly on the lone remaining wall. In the distance I can hear the wail of approaching aid.

There's something indecent about glimpsing someone's private space after a midnight bomb has shattered it. Flash of wallpaper. The wind shuffling the pages of an open book. All that was not meant for us to see, suddenly all there is to see. Just as the taxi pulls away from this crater of rubble, I see the hand. It pokes out from a pile of broken bricks, fingers curled slightly as though it has just thrown a ball and is waiting to catch it as it falls from the sky. A child's hand. I see the sleeve of fabric still attached, and then the taxi is past.

I do not know how to reconcile myself to useless random death. I do not know how to assimilate this much brutal change, or how to relearn this landscape that was once so familiar to me and is now different every day. I cannot find my way back to my life when all my known landmarks are being removed. Last week I even became lost in the corner of Bloomsbury where I lived before I moved to Mrs. Royce's on Denbigh Street at the beginning of the war, to be closer to my office. I was looking for my usual marker that determined where to turn, a four-storey brick house on the corner of a square. The house had become, since last I'd been there, a small hill of brick dust and broken glass.

This is what I know about love. That it is tested every day, and what is not renewed is lost. One chooses either to care more or to care less. Once the choice is to care less, then there is no stopping the momentum of goodbye. Each loved thing slips away. There is no stopping it.

We have arrived at Paddington. The sun shivers along the glass in the station roof.

So long, sweetheart.

2

One of the worst things about the war has been the paranoia about being invaded by the enemy. This has been directly translated into making travel as difficult as possible for all civilians, on the odd chance there might be a spy among us, sent ahead to gain information on where to invade first. To confuse these spies, all the signs in rural England have been removed. No markers for villages or towns. No signs at the train stations. Children have been strictly cautioned to never answer any stranger who begs for directions, and there are posters up everywhere warning that "Careless Talk Costs Lives." No one seems to have considered that a spy might come equipped with a map.

It is difficult to set out for somewhere new. The concession the railway has made to people such as myself, who are travelling to an unfamiliar location, is to attach a small, practically invisible label bearing the station's name to the base of a lamp standard at the far end of the platform. Unless you are in the first carriage and it is daylight and you lean half your body out of the window and have remarkably good eyesight, the label is impossible to see. It is completely impossible at night, when all the lights in the train are routinely turned off and the darkened carriage-loads of people hurtle through the unknown landscape to certain geographical distress.

The war has made us all nervous, jittery rabbits. I look on my fellow train travellers with sympathy. No one had expected the war to last so long, and now, with Hitler poised to invade Yugoslavia and Rommel launching a desert offensive, it seems more widespread and endless than ever—more hopeless than ever. The effort of the citizenry to remain alive and alert to all possible danger has transformed us all into twitchy, apprehensive, exhausted creatures.

"I was counting," says the woman opposite me to her

husband. "But now I can't remember if it's five or six stations we've passed."

I was counting too, and when she says this, I immediately can't remember either. The train plunges further southwest towards the Devon countryside, and I realize that probably no one in this carriage has the faintest idea where we are.

The man doesn't reply to his wife's irritation. He is ignoring her. This is how I know they are married. He turns his newspaper over, and I read the front page of *The Times*. "Half Abyssinia Conquered" one of the headlines says, and then, under that, I spot something that makes me lean forward in my seat.

"We announce with regret that it must now be presumed that Mrs. Leonard Woolf (Virginia Woolf, the novelist and essayist), who has been missing since last Friday, has been drowned in the Sussex Ouse at Rodmell, near Lewes."

I think of the letter I was writing in my head this morning to Mrs. Woolf. *This felt moment. Our brief selves.* All the letters I write in my head. All the letters never perfect enough to actually send. And now I've missed my chance to let her know how much I have loved her books, and to tell her that one evening, seven years ago, I think I followed her through the streets of London. Now the answer to the question I was always on the brink of asking—*Was it you?*—will never be known to me.

I remember that the moon was up, and that when I crossed Tavistock Square the gardens were flooded with light. It took me a while even to notice the tall shadowy figure of a woman, walking ahead of me through the gardens of the square. But when I did notice her, it was as if I also noticed everything else for the first time. The June air was soft on my skin, and the watery flume of traffic streaming by in the Southampton Row was suddenly hushed. The air smelled of flowering trees and that scent was the scent of possibility, of hopefulness.

There is a vocabulary to existing, to taking up living space in the world, that cannot be translated over the chasm of death.

I saw the tall, slightly stooped figure of Virginia Woolf walking through the night square in a flowing dress the colour of dusk. What words can I possibly use to truly cover this experience?

A mauve dress. The colour of lilacs. It hangs around the body, drapes it like smoke, ghostly in the rise of moonlight over the London houses. We were alive. We were on fire. I sit in this rocking train carriage, years later, words floating around me, wisping down in thin, grey threads. Nothing I can hold in my hands. Smoke, these words are smoke.

I rest my head on the window. I can see a faint image of my face in the glass, through it the countryside churns a soft green. Strange to see fields again, trees knotted above water, a kingfisher over the river. No ruined buildings, air thick with masonry dust. Strange also to see my face again, in the train window. I don't often gaze at my reflection.

When my mother knew she was dying, she made me remove all the mirrors from her house, stack them in the conservatory, glass to the wall. "I don't expect you'll want them," she said.

I lift my head from the window. I have left her too,

my dead mother. She belongs with the burning city, the ash and broken stone of London. Her house was bombed while she was in hospital. That house in Richmond I grew up in. "I wish I'd been there," she said when I told her.

A few rows ahead of me in the carriage I can see the uniformed arm of a soldier. The rest of his body is hidden by the seat. I suddenly feel completely miserable. This is all I have—a carriage full of strangers, a landscape disarmingly lush and unfamiliar, memories that bring no comfort.

3

There is no one to meet me at the small country station, even though, when I first made the arrangements, someone had been promised. Another example of the rampant unreliability this war has wrought on even the simplest of promises. "There's a war on," people will say to explain away almost any behaviour.

I was told the estate was not far from the train station, and if my luggage were not so heavy, I would attempt to walk the distance. But the weight of my books necessitates transport. I do not have much for being thirty-five years on this earth: mostly books, a few photographs. My clothes are few. But my books, my books are so many it looks as though I am on my way to open a small lending library.

A ride is easier to come by than I would have thought. A Canadian captain is picking up one of his men at the station—the soldier who was seated several rows in front of me on the train.

"Give you a lift, ma'am?" he asks me. I am dragging my bags across the station platform, the effort of this taking so much time that there is now no one on the station platform except for the soldiers and myself.

"Thank you, yes. I'm going to Mosel."

"That's easy, then. So are we." The captain is tall and fair-haired. When he bends down to grab my bags there is a faint murmur of alcohol on his breath.

"What are you doing there?" I say, rather rudely, I know, but I had been told only that the estate had been requisitioned for food production. There had been no mention of soldiers.

The fair-haired Canadian heaves my bags into the rear of the motor car. "We're billeted there," he says, holding the door open for me. "In the house. Waiting to be posted. And you?" He looks at me then, really looks at me, and I lower my eyes.

"Posted," I say. It sounds better than saying I volunteered. "I have come down from London to supervise the gardens."

"You're with the Land Girls, then?" He shuts the door on me and lets himself into the driver's seat. "There's quite a pack of them up there already."

"But they weren't meant to arrive until next week." I was supposed to have had time to inspect the grounds and formulate a work schedule. "They're not meant to be there at all."

"Well, then, they're imposters, but there are certainly

some Land Girls on the estate," the captain says cheerfully. The soldier from the train climbs into the front passenger seat and we begin our drive away from the station, up the long, winding hill to Mosel.

The estate is larger and more separate from the small town than I had imagined. I am glad I didn't attempt to walk when I see the long steep hill that leads towards it. There is a river at the bottom of the hill. I think of Mrs. Woolf. "There's a river," I say, rather pointlessly.

"Stream," says the fair-haired soldier, who has just told me his name is Raley.

"Brook," says the other one. This is the first word he's spoken since getting off the train.

"That's because he's from Newfoundland," says Raley. "Right, David?" He nudges his fellow soldier with his elbow.

"Well, it *is* a brook," says David again. "I can't help it if you'll be getting it wrong, Captain Raley. Sir," he adds as an afterthought.

I bristle a little at the insubordination, but Raley just grins.

Ascending from the river, elms line the sides of the driveway. Through them I can see the tidy fields. Beyond the fields, woods. The elms have been very purposefully planted to funnel the gaze forward up the rise of hill, up and up into the angled blue sky.

"Here you go, then." Raley stops the car abruptly, and both David and I lurch forward in our seats and then lurch backwards again.

We have stopped in front of a stone archway. Through the archway I can see a clipped square of lawn, what must be the centre of a quadrangle.

Raley carries my bags effortlessly out of the car and deposits them on the cobbles under the arch. "Shall I bring them in for you, ma'am?" He is unfailingly polite. I can't tell how genuine he is from this one brief meeting, but I am grateful for his care of me.

"Thank you, but I think I can manage from here." The truth is that although I am tired from my journey, I want to see this place for the first time by myself. "And if I can't, I'll find an imposter to assist me."

Raley smiles at me. "Come and see us sometime," he says. "We're just up the hill." He is very handsome and he knows it. I can tell that. He is the kind of man who gets pleasure out of watching himself be chivalrous and charming to an unattractive older woman.

"Thank you." I shake his hand, which is clean and strong. No dirt under his nails.

"Good luck, then." Raley waves as he gets back into the motorcar. David has remained in the passenger seat throughout our little farewell, looking straight ahead and clutching his small rucksack to his chest. He does not appear overjoyed to be back at Mosel.

I leave my bags on the cobbles and step through the archway into sudden sunlight, and my first look at the place that will change my life forever.

Everything is larger than was expected. I stand on the strict, flat lawn. To the right is a two-storey wing, windows at regular intervals. To my left is a small barn, and attached to that, running the whole left side of the quadrangle, are low, stone stables. Ahead, at the bottom of the quad, is a fancier version of what is on the right-hand side, which must have been apartments or rooms for the employees of the stables and gardens. The gardens are nowhere in sight.

There is a gravel path around the grassy rectangle. All along the edges of the path, up against the grey stone of the buildings, I can see what is left of an impressive mixed border.

This estate was originally made to function very efficiently. A closed world of human industry. The odd thing about standing here now is that I am the only person in this courtyard. Where is everyone? Perhaps that soldier was wrong about his sightings of the Women's Land Army.

I abandon my luggage and go in search of people, starting with the grander portion of the quad opposite me, across the stretch of lawn. Each of the stone steps up to the heavy wooden doorway is worn in the middle into a smooth hollow. All those years of weight in the same place, like a promise kept and kept and kept.

There's no one to be found in this building. Downstairs there's an enormous kitchen. Upstairs a cavernous dining hall with a massive fireplace at one end and huge, leaded windows, as grand as a church's. I stand at one of the windows and look out over what seems to be the gardens. Overgrown yews take up the foreground. Beyond the yews I can see the large enclosed rectangle of what must be a kitchen garden. There is a tangle of greenery over the brick walls. The grounds are much bigger than I had originally supposed. All around the kitchen garden are clusters of shrubs, signs perhaps of other smaller gardens. There are hills and hollows to the right. To the left, the flat scrape of fields leading down to the river.

For an estate of this size, there must be an orchard. I scan the landscape around the kitchen garden for the telltale twist of apple trees, but there is so much untended and overgrown that I cannot single out any fruit trees from the mess of trees and shrubs.

I keep remembering that Virginia Woolf died. But it didn't actually say *died* in that article in the *Times*. It said *presumed*, which means they have not found the body. Her body.

The sun emerges from behind a cloud and anchors the great, unruly yews to the lawn by their shadows.

There must be a way that the dining hall connects to the west wing, but I can't find it and have to go back outside to re-enter the right side of the quadrangle. The first floor of the long, stone building is broken up into various useful areas—vast cupboards containing linens and blankets, a laundry, a room full of coal scuttles. Upstairs are lavatories, two baths—one at each end of the lengthy hallway—and a series of bedrooms. All the bedrooms appear to be under ownership. I open the door of each room and see clothes strewn over the furniture or hung neatly in the wardrobes. In one of the rooms there's a stuffed animal on the bed, a rather threadbare dog with a single glass eye in its plush head. Another of the rooms contains yards of fabric draped over a chair. Silk. I touch the soft slipperiness of it and think of the flicker of sleeve I glimpsed this morning from the taxi. The sleeve. The hand.

I move down the hallway. There's a room with music books, and a room with a very neatly made bed. Beside the bed, on a small white table, is a photograph of a young man in an RAF uniform. He has his arms crossed in a casual manner, but his face is unsmiling, and has a hungry look that could be tiredness, or fear. I don't know why I do it, but I touch his face with my finger, gently, the way one touches something very delicate. The thin crepe skin of a poppy. A wineglass with a spidery web of lines breaching its surface.

Finally, near the end of the hall, at the part of the building that is closest to where the Canadian soldiers dropped me and where my luggage still waits, there is an empty room. There's a wardrobe and a dresser, a basin, a bed near the dormer window that looks down into the courtyard and beyond to the stables opposite. There's a small fireplace and a great arch of old timber that obviously supports the roof. It is carved up and battered, as though it grew here, open to the elements, long before there was a building for it to hold up.

I open the dresser drawers and the wardrobe doors. Nothing. I stand in the centre of this room, which might, if unclaimed, be mine, and notice that there's a particular odour. The room smells as though it has recently been on fire, although there's no physical evidence anywhere to support this. But the smell of burning is unmistakable. I go out into the hall, where it smells like a normal musty, damp building, and then go back into the room where it smells like scorched wood.

Out in the hall again, I finally see another human being—a young woman, hurtling at great speed towards me.

"Hello," I say. She skids to a stop. She is small and dark, slight, under a layer of jerseys.

"Hello," she says. "You're new." She doesn't wait for me to answer, peers into my new room. "Oh, right," she says. "No one wanted this one. It stinks."

"What happened?"

The jersey girl shrugs. "Mystery," she says. "Human sacrifice. Cooking gone disastrously wrong."

It's all a mystery. Where anyone is. Who they are. Why nothing has aligned with the written information I received when I volunteered for this position.

"Who are you, then?" I say. I have lost patience with all this.

"Jane." She looks hard at me, meeting my impatience with a certain strictness of her own. "Who are you?"

"Gwen Davis. From the Royal Horticultural Society."

"The Royal what?"

"Horticultural Society." I say it very slowly, as though I'm talking to an imbecile. I can't believe she hasn't heard of it. We're famous. Our reputation extends all over the world. At least, I think it does.

"What did you do there? At the Horticultural Society." She draws out every syllable of the last two words, mimicking me.

"I was working for the Fruits and Vegetables Committee."

"Doing what?"

"Trying to find a cure for parsnip canker."

The truth is that I was nowhere near a cure of any sort. This is part of the reason I wanted the job here, taking charge of the wartime agricultural production of a requisitioned country estate, because I was failing so abysmally at my real work. For months now I had been meticulously observing parsnip canker. I had made copious notes. I had many specimens. But I could not bridge the chasm between my long row of parsnips in the laboratory, all in various stages of fetid death, and the remedy that might exist for all this rotted vegetable flesh on the opposite shore of science. Or miracle.

Jane looks at me, then suddenly grins and skips quickly down the staircase.

"Dinner's at seven," she calls up from the bottom. "Sorry about your cancer."

4

The best gardens are a perfect balance of order and chaos. The tension created by this constantly threatened balance is the pulse of the garden itself.

I have not worked in many gardens since my time at the Royal Horticultural Society. And since my observation of vegetable canker began a year ago I have not even seen much besides my ward of terminally ill parsnips. But I only have to open the door of the walled kitchen garden to know that this is a garden in complete chaos.

There is a cross of weeds, once a path, dividing the large expanse of ground into four equal parts. At one time this vegetable garden must have been organized around a classic four-year crop rotation. It could be that, under the weeds and bits of debris, the soil is still healthy.

I kneel down at the edge of a bed, push my hands beneath a tangle of dead tree branches into the cool, moist earth.

All of today has felt unreal to me. Leaving the boarding house—which I can't quite bring myself to call my home, though it is where I have lived for the past two years. Leaving the city I adore. The train journey down to the West Country. The news about Mrs. Woolf. The oddness of this place, where there is evidence of other people, but only that one rude girl named Jane to be found. None of it has seemed to belong to my experience of life at all. And now, for the first time today, with my hands full of rich, clotted earth, I actually feel attached to my life again.

I rub the dirt between my fingers. The red earth of Devon is thick and full of texture. I put a little on the tip of my tongue and taste the wormy, metallic tang of soil choked with nutrients. It will be fine. All will be fine. I tilt my head back to the sun and close my eyes. I have missed this, forgotten how much I love to be down on the ground among the living things, my hands plunged up to the wrists in the sweet, sticky earth. I am a gardener who has essentially been indoors for the past ten years. Where's the sense in that?

There's the cheerful song of a bird in a tree by the garden wall. When was the last time I heard a bird in London? Here, the war seems not to exist at all. It is too far west for the drone of bombers on their way over the Channel. Was there a world like this before the war? A quiet world. A slow garden.

Suddenly I can remember birds in Green Park, before the war, when I had walked down from my lodgings in Bloomsbury, on my way to work in Vincent

Square. Birds in Green Park. Birds in Russell Square. Trees pooled in daffodils. I could thread myself through London moving from leafy square to leafy square.

There's an old chicken coop and run against one of the garden walls. A small brick shed against another of the walls. The door is secured with a rusted padlock and the window too sheeted with grime to see through. It bears further examination, this building. There might be tools in its dark confines. I'll have to return later with something to pry the lock off.

As I'm leaving the garden I meet another girl, hurrying past the wall towards the entrance of the quadrangle. She's as big as Jane was small, has a strong, lumbering gait, and masses of curly hair that bounce with each huge stride. She looks a bit like a giant child, has her head down, doesn't see me at all. I stand in her path and she very nearly knocks me over.

"Stop." I put my hand out.

"Sorry." She seems utterly surprised to see me.

"What is going on here?" I say. I take my hand away from her shoulder and see the smudge of dirt I've left on her cardigan. "I have come down from London to take charge of a group of agricultural workers, none of whom are meant to be here yet, and when I arrive it appears that all the girls are already here. But I can't find anyone. What is going on?"

The big girl seems genuinely frightened by my outburst. She steps backwards. I step forward. She steps backwards again, and we proceed in a strange, halting dance along the path towards the garden. Finally she backs into the wall. "They're all up at the house, ma'am."

"What house?"

"The house full of Canadian soldiers."

"And what are the girls doing there?"

"Visiting."

"Visiting?" I can't believe the nerve. "This is a war, not a Sunday outing," I say, although with the sunshine and the bucolic fug of nature, it really does more closely resemble a Sunday picnic.

The big girl looks down at her shoes. So do I. They are huge shoes, man-size. "I'm sorry," she says. "We didn't know what to do. There didn't seem to be anyone in charge."

"Well, I'm in charge. And I'm here now. I want you to go back up to the house and tell the others to get down here. No more visiting. There's work to be started. I will speak to everyone at dinner tonight."

"Yes, ma'am." The big girl sidles along the brick wall towards the quadrangle. This is the opposite direction from where I believe the house is.

"Where are you going?" I can't believe, after her submissive attitude, she would so soon disobey me.

"To the house."

"Isn't the house that way?" I point past the garden, up the hill.

"There's a shortcut behind the west wing. A path through the woods."

"How long have you been here?" What if the Land Girls have been at Mosel for weeks? What chance will I ever have to gain control over them?

"Four days."

"And you already know a shortcut to the house?" This is all much worse than I had thought. The girls have probably moved in with the soldiers.

"I'm local." The big girl looks at me with a small flash of confidence. "My father used to work here. In the gardens. I know this place."

This is a stroke of good fortune. Deciphering the garden will be easier if there is someone who is familiar with it to help me.

"Is your father still alive?" I ask.

"Yes."

"And does he live nearby?"

"In the village." The big girl thinks I'm on the track of something else. "I could stay there, ma'am, I know that, but I've never had a chance to be away from home before. And to stay at Mosel is so exciting."

I could remind her that we're staying in what were probably the servants' quarters, and that staying on an estate such as this only truly counts if one is living in the main house, but there is no point being deliberately cruel. I need this girl. She will prove useful.

"Of course, you can continue to stay here," I say. "Just go and fetch the others from the house. I'll see you all at dinner."

I have been touched three times in my life. Intentionally touched. Firstly by my mother, although I don't remember much affection when I was small and certainly none after I was sent away to school. The second instance was at boarding school. It involved a fellow student. I was fourteen years old. The third time of purposeful physical contact was with Mr. Gregory, under the makeshift bomb shelter of the dining-room table at Mrs. Royce's London boarding house.

One's first experience of love is either love received or love denied, and against that experience all our future desires and expectations are measured.

My mother touched me on the head. She said, "At least you have beautiful hair." She rubbed my chest with liniment. My mother held my hand one year when I was afraid of the bull in the back field, and wouldn't hold it the following year, even though I was still afraid. She wiped the crumbs from my lips. "Learn to cover your mouth," she said. Once she brushed the rain from my forehead. She spanked me. She pulled my arm too hard trying to make me keep up with her. She slapped my hand away from the cakes at tea. She dressed me. She undressed me. She soaped me in the bath, rubbed my scalp fiercely when washing it, clipped my toenails impatiently with rusty scissors. The last time I saw her, when she was small and sick and dying in the hospital, she held my head in her bony, shaky hands and said, "At least you are useful."

My school friend was called Anna. Every night for one whole month when we were fourteen she slipped out of her bed after there was "lights out" in the dormitory, and slipped into mine. It was January. I never knew if our temporary intimacy was due to the fact that it was an unusually cold winter, or if it was motivated by some other desire that I was afraid to want, but wanted anyway. Every night Anna would lift the covers of my narrow bed and snuggle in behind me. She would nuzzle under my hair and kiss the back of my neck. Her nose was as cold as a dog's. She would lie on her right arm and drape her left around my waist. Once I held her hand, held it tight against my stomach. Once she said my name out loud, like a promise. Then, just as I had become used to the nightly ritual, it ended. Anna stayed in her own bed and left me in mine. Perhaps she had been cautioned by a teacher, or perhaps she simply tired of me. I was never brave enough to ask.

Mr. Gregory always saved me a spot next to him on the hard wooden floor of the dining room. At night, with the blackout curtains drawn tight to the windows, the room was as dark as the inside of the earth. Mr. Gregory licked my ear, mistaking it, I think, for my mouth. He rubbed my knee with a sweaty hand. He cleared his throat, seemed just about to say something of significance, but never said it. Once he did say, "Sorry," but this might have been because he rubbed Mrs. Royce's knee instead of mine and realized, too late, that her lumpy cartilage didn't feel familiar under his hand. Mr. Gregory burrowed up against me only in the dark, a sticky, sweaty nocturnal creature with nervous, moist, blind desires.

No one has ever said that they love me. Well, only my mother, but it was a defensive statement in response to my accusation that she didn't. "Of course I love you," she had said. "I look after you, don't I?"

It is almost time for dinner and I am afraid to go. I have never been good at dealing with people. I much prefer to work alone. This position at Mosel had seemed possible because I was to have arrived well ahead of the Land Girls and I would be much older and more experienced than they were. The combination of these factors would ensure my authority without my having to prove or test it. But all has gone badly awry because the girls have arrived here well before me and so this place rightfully belongs to them. I am the intruder. For me to march into the dining room tonight and take charge will surely engender their immediate dislike of me, and perhaps even their unwillingness to follow any instruction at all. They have had a few days of complete freedom, have formed God-knows-what kinds of alliances with the soldiers. How can I possibly get them on my side now?

I liked my job at the Royal Horticultural Society because I had such autonomy. It was just me and the parsnips locked in deathly combat in my narrow little office on the ground floor at the back of the building near to where the dustbins were kept. On summer days, with my window open, I could smell the rubbish quite strongly, often mistaking it for the odours of my parsnip specimens. But I was left alone there. I did not have to fuss with people, only parsnips.

I almost didn't apply for this position with the Women's Land Army. A letter had circulated through the Royal Horticultural Society from the WLA head office and had, at some point, crossed my desk. The letter asked for volunteers who had knowledge of agricultural production and horticulture to supervise the growing of food for the war effort. Postings could be anywhere in arable Britain. The letter coincided with the "Dig for Victory" campaign, where citizens were requested to transform their flower gardens into plots for growing potatoes. There were posters all around London, and I found the slogan mildly annoying as it left out many steps of the process of growing and harvesting vegetables. I also didn't approve of the illustration that accompanied the phrase "Dig for Victory." A booted foot pushing a spade blade into the earth. The whole approach seemed much more to do with the war than gardening. But then everything connected with the war had become necessarily tainted by it. Everything connected with the war had become the war itself.

Every step I take across the quadrangle, every step that takes me closer to the dining hall, fills me with a heavy despair. I never wanted to be in charge of a group of girls. I am no good at this sort of thing. I just wanted to be out of London before it was bombed beyond recognition. I wanted to escape the inevitable decline of my parsnip specimens.

I can hear the girls giggling as I climb the wide stone steps up into the dining hall. There is nothing to be done but to face this. I take a deep breath and push open the studded oak door to the room.

Heavy blackout curtains are pulled across the windows where I had stood earlier, looking down into the gardens. The girls are sitting at one long table in front of the fireplace. They are completely silent as I enter the room, cross the floor towards them.

There are seven of them, including Jane. They all seem as young as the big girl I met outside the garden this afternoon. Jane is the only one of them who seems older than twenty, and she is certainly no more than twenty-five. There is an empty chair beside her at the head of the table and I slide into it. No one speaks. The heavy curtains at the windows muffle any sound from outdoors. There's the small, shifting noise of something trickling down the chimney.

Jane looks at me with what might be sympathy or pity. "Girls," she says. "Meet Gwen Davis. From the Horticultural Society." She draws out the last two words for my benefit. Her mockery makes me flinch.

"Hello," I say to the table of impassive faces. "It's good to meet you."

The girls regard me suspiciously.

"Don't mind them," says Jane. "They've taken a vow of hostility. It's something to do in the evenings."

This brings a smile to several of the faces. I realize, from Jane's position at the head of the table and from her easy manner, that she has had unofficial charge of the girls. She is the natural leader of this little group.

I want to say something to her to indicate my acknowledgement of this observation, but I can't find the right words. To the girls at the table I say, "There seems to have been a mix-up. You were meant to arrive after I got here."

No response from the girls. There's the noise of someone scuffing her shoes on the piece of floor under her chair.

The sooner I can get this over with the better. "Anyway, I'm here now," I say needlessly, but I am so overcome with nerves that I feel completely muddled and don't know where to start. I am not very good with groups. Something I should have thought about, really, before volunteering for this job.

"I'll brief you, shall I?" says Jane. She touches my arm

lightly, to stop me from saying anything further. "In your much regretted absence," she says, "the county rep was by. Her name is Mrs. Billings. She dropped off our uniforms, which include, I must add, a very unfortunate sort of hat. I have your allotment of clothes. I'll give them to you after supper." As if on cue, the dining-hall doors open and two women enter carrying plates of food. The big girl giggles. Jane is unfazed. "Supper," she says. "These lovely women have been hired from the village to cook our evening meal for us." She waves a hand theatrically in their direction. "Mabel," she says, as the elder of the women places a plate of what looks like animal swill before one of the girls. "Irene," she says, as the other woman performs the same task. Both of the women look up and smile in a kind of alarmed embarrassment. "We're on our own for breakfast and lunch," Jane says to me.

"What about money?" I say.

"I'll show you the coffers." Jane grimaces as her plate of food is placed in front of her. "There's money from the War Agricultural Committee." She pokes at the lump of grey gristle floating in watery gravy on her plate. "There's also money from the people who own this estate, to pay for the upkeep of the animals."

"Animals? What animals?" There was no mention to me of there being any animals to look after at Mosel.

"Some cows. Two horses." Jane puts her knife and fork down without eating any of her food. "That's what I've decided to do here. Tend the animals." There is no room in her voice for disagreement. Nor would I try. It is obvious that Jane is much more of a commanding presence than I am. She knows how to lead effortlessly.

These girls are not going to be swayed by my horticultural knowledge alone. If I am to have any chance with them, if I am to gain their obedience and trust, I must lead with a light hand. Perhaps the best way to lead is not to appear to be leading at all.

I wait until all the girls have their plates of supper and Mabel and Irene have left the dining hall. "I only have a few words to add," I say. "Please, go ahead and eat while I talk." I am desperate now to cooperate with them in whatever way is possible to make this situation more bearable. "As you know, we are here to work the garden, and to use some of the surrounding land for potatoes. We're all here to pitch in with the hoe." I have forgotten the exact words but I am referring to the official Land Army song, which tries to make up for our lack of weaponry by glorifying the hoe.

No one responds to my attempt at humour. All the girls stare at me fixedly, their hands holding their cutlery raised above their food in suspended animation. I look at the big girl. "What's your name?"

"Doris."

"Is anyone besides Doris local?" I ask.

No one responds. Finally Jane says, "They're mostly from London."

"All right, then," I say. "Tomorrow after breakfast we'll meet in the walled kitchen garden. I will outline the work detail and Doris will be in charge of it."

"I will?" Doris looks at me in horror.

"You will. That's all until then. Obviously, you've managed well enough before I arrived. I'll leave you to your own devices this evening. But please, no leaving the grounds. No visiting the soldiers who are billeted at the house." I load some of what I'm guessing is mutton stew onto my fork, and the girls follow my example and start eating. Soon they are talking among themselves, ignoring me completely. Only Doris pays any attention to my presence, keeps shooting me little looks of panic.

Jane has pushed away her full plate of food. She watches me eat my supper. "Interesting tactic," she says, in a voice meant only for me to hear. "Separating the potatoes from the potatoes."

6

After supper has been cleared and several of the girls have gone to do the washing-up, I head downstairs with Jane to collect my Land Army uniform from the cupboard by the laundry room.

She hands out items of clothing. There are many more pieces of apparel involved in being a Land Girl than I had anticipated.

"Two green jerseys. Two pairs of breeches. Two pairs of dungarees." Jane hurls these at me in rapid succession. "The size might not be right, but there are extras in here to sort through, and someone else might swap with you. Look at this." She waves something in front of my nose. It's the hat, a limp fold of felt. Jane tosses it on top of the pile in my arms. "Not even fit to be a tea cosy," she says.

I watch Jane in the cupboard, shirts and trousers

swirling around her like weather. I want to ask her about the other girls, about what's been happening here in my absence, but her energy leaves me speechless. A mackintosh flies out of the cupboard and drapes itself over one of my shoulders. There seems to be no end to these clothes. "Why are there so many things?" I say.

Jane kicks a pair of wellingtons towards me. "It's hard to stay clean and look smart," she says. "In such a healthy, happy job."

I recognize this line from a Women's Land Army recruitment poster. It's almost as bad as the song about the hoe.

"Why are you here?" I ask.

Jane removes the rain hat she's jammed on her head and looks straight at me. "Why do you ask?"

"You don't seem like the others."

"Thank God." She throws the rain hat onto the peak of my clothing mountain and fishes a packet of Gold Flakes out from a jersey pocket. "Cadged them off a soldier," she says. She offers the package to me and I shake my head no. "You're right." She lights a cigarette, inhales deeply, exhales a stream of smoke at the stacks of carefully folded bed linens. "I'm not here for a big adventure. Or to 'do my bit.'"

"Then, why are you here?"

"I grew up on a farm. My parents thought it would be a good environment for me to return to. Especially now."

The cupboard is getting very smoky. I back out into the hallway and Jane follows me. "Why now?" I say. We lean against the hall wall, facing each other. I rest my chin on the heap of clothing in my arms.

"Because I'm in distress. That's what the doctors call it. The ones they took me to see. Distress." Jane leans her head against the wall. There's a blue vein pulsing in her left temple. The fingernails on her hand lifting the cigarette to her mouth are bitten down to the bleeding point. "And it's true, I suppose," she says. "I have a fiancé who's missing. Andrew. 'Missing in action,' they call it. Since March the fifth."

This makes me think of Virginia Woolf. Missing in action. That's exactly what's happened to her. She seems definitely to be a casualty of war at the moment. Like any other.

When I used to work more actively in private gardens I was always criticized for how slowly I developed a new one. I was a very slow planter. I liked to plant one kind of flower at a time, giving it a season or two to expand into whatever space it required. Living things know what they need. I have always thought this. Why crowd something from the start, when it has had no chance yet even to become itself? Gardening, which needs patience, is often the domain of the impatient. I was sometimes not kept on in those private gardens, where the desire was for instant beauty.

I could ask Jane all the questions of curiosity and concern. But I don't. I lean against the wall and watch her smoke her cigarette. The oily canvas of the rain hat is sticking to my chin. I am suddenly very tired. This war has gone on for so long, I think, that this endless waiting is life now. There is nothing else. "Sometimes, I think that everything we always wanted comes to us in the disguise of this war. What are we waiting for? We're waiting to recover. We're waiting to go home. We're waiting for someone to return to us. Solace and love. What else is there?" I realize, too late, that I've said this out loud.

Jane looks at me intently. "Are those our choices?" she says.

"Yes, I think so."

"What are you waiting for, Gwen?"

I am embarrassed by having said so much to this stranger, but I am too weary to stop now. "Love," I say. It is the truth, and I have never said it out loud. "And you?"

Jane's voice is soft, quiet, as though the wisps of smoke she breathes out are the words gone from her body. "I'm waiting for love too," she says. "I'm waiting for the love I had to come back to me."

I remember the room in the west wing I'd walked into earlier, the one with the photograph of the airman by the bed. How he looked both edgy and at ease. How I had touched his face. That must be Andrew. "Love," I say again, because now that I have admitted it, I cannot stop confessing.

7

Of all my books that I have dragged down to Devon from London, the grandest is *The Genus Rosa.* Miss Willmott's encyclopedia of roses is in two volumes, each huge and heavy, weighted down with her botanical earnestness. I haul them from my luggage, lie on the floor, and pull one volume onto my chest, one onto my stomach. I did this in London when the German bombing became more frenzied this past winter. Actually I started the ritual of comfort a few months before that, when my mother was dying in hospital.

I lie under *The Genus Rosa* on the floor of this, my temporary home. I can see all the dust under the bed next to me. The room still smells strongly of fire. The books press down on me. Surely no one could weigh as much as *The Genus Rosa*? But this is what I imagine—someone. This is what I think about—love.

The Genus Rosa was the only gift my mother ever gave me. The only gift I truly appreciated. The size and heft of it would have suited her fondness for theatricality. As a gesture, it was superb. She gave it to me when I graduated from gardening college. The books were so heavy she couldn't carry them into the hall, had to pull me from the reception to come and fetch them from her car. But I didn't mind, not when I saw *The Genus Rosa* sitting on the back seat of the Austin. "There," she said, flinging open the door. "Isn't that the most fabulous present?" And it was. It was. Perhaps I have never been as happy as I was that day. I remember the sharp smell of the leather seats, my hand on the smooth side of the car as I leaned in. And there it was, *The Genus Rosa*, propped up against the seat back, each volume as sturdy as the wall of a small house.

I am only a few years older than the first volume of *The Genus Rosa*. I like thinking that when I was born, Miss Willmott was deep in the writing of it. Was there a particular rose she was working on the exact moment of my birth? The *Arvensis* perhaps, or the *Phoenicea*? Maybe even the *Rosa rugosa* itself. I like to think that the moment I first breathed in the air of this world was the moment Ellen Willmott wrote *Rosa rugosa* at the top of a blank piece of paper.

8

Dear Mrs. Woolf.

Of your books, I must say that I like *To the Lighthouse* best of all. It is a perfect garden. The right mix of order and chaos. I admire (No) I love how the lighthouse, always in the background of the story, is to some extent Mrs. Ramsay herself. How the strokes of light are part of the emotional rhythm of Mrs. Ramsay.

I would say (No) Is it true, perhaps, that this book is really about the haunting of memory? This is also what makes it a perfect garden because that's what flowers are sometimes to us, ghosts.

Did you once walk through Tavistock Square, seven years ago now, in June? This is what haunts me. And now that you are lost. (No) Now that you've gone missing, I might never know your answer.

I liked in *To the Lighthouse* that the big questions Mr. Ramsay asked, about art and civilization, were directed to the escallonia hedge.

But I am thinking now of Tavistock Square, of London. I cannot go on with this letter in my head, this endless letter I go on thinking up and never actually send. And why do I continue to do this when the person to whom I would send it is perhaps not even still living? Habit? Need? Because it links me to that night in June seven years ago, when there was no war, when all the buildings were still in place on my particular route through the city. How I would link London up for myself as a series of green squares on the way to the river. Sunlight on grass. The white stone of the city churches against the night sky. Like bones, I could say they were like bones. I could say the city was a body I pressed to mine. The fine hair of the tall grasses in Highgate Cemetery. The smell of the river. That world as it was, that I will never inhabit again.

9

I locate the letter from the Women's Land Army head office as I'm putting my books and clothes away in my new room. When I open it and read through it, I find that the mistake has all been mine. I was meant to have arrived at Mosel a week ago. Somehow I had muddled the date. No wonder there was no one to meet me at the station.

I sit down on my bed, the letter in hand. How could I have been so foolish? All the disorganization of today is my fault and could have been avoided.

"Why are you such an idiot?" my mother used to say

to me when I'd failed to grasp some adult nuance. It always felt like such an unfair question. If I was such an idiot, how would I be able to answer that?

I had wanted a new start. I had wanted a return to gardening. I had wanted to be useful and liked for what I knew. Now I had ruined my chances before I'd even begun. I crumple up the letter and hurl it at the wardrobe.

Outside the air is cool, prickles a little on my skin as I walk out into the quadrangle. No wardens here. No screech of bombs, clatter of bricks falling. I tilt my head back to see the stars, but the gesture makes me feel so lonely I almost start to cry. "Idiot," I say, instead. "You're such an idiot."

I walk slowly along the gravel path that borders the quadrangle. It has been so long since I walked anywhere at night with such ease of purpose. If I was in London walking at night, in these days of the Blitz, I would, at some point, have to hurl myself dramatically down some shop's cellar stairs, or scurry home to burrow under Mrs. Royce's dining table.

As I walk around by the stables I hear a noise. It's a noise I unfortunately recognize from Mr. Gregory, whose room next to mine on Denbigh Street was separated only by a regrettably thin wall. I push open the stable door and see them lying on the straw. They are thankfully both still dressed. "What are you doing?" I say loudly, even though it is perfectly clear what it is they are doing.

There is a mad scramble and they unexpectedly shoot past me, clutching their undone pieces of clothing to their bodies. The soldier. The Land Army girl. In the darkness I can't get a good look at the girl as they're now running across the quadrangle. The worst thing of all is that they're laughing. I close the stable door firmly behind them. I would lock it if I could, but there's no lock.

I continue my walk around the quadrangle. I feel too shaken to go back to my room and don't know what else to do. After my third time around the courtyard I tire of this and head out into the darker surround of the kitchen garden. I run my hands along the brick wall beside me, remembering how I felt my way along Denbigh Street one night when there was no moon. House to house, each dark stone smooth under my hand, until I reached the iron railing that bordered Mrs. Royce's house. How I never turned a light on once inside, felt my way up the staircase to my room, undressed in the dark, slid into bed—as though the whole journey was the same moment, extended and unbroken. It is light that dismantles each moment, I had thought then. Light proves it one thing or another. Darkness does not judge.

I have reached the end of the garden wall. Just as I turn the corner to continue walking around the wall there's a scream. A young woman materializes ahead of me in the darkness.

"What?" I say. The scream has startled me and I stub my hand against the bricks. It is a Land Army girl. I can't tell if it's the same one I just caught in the barn with the soldier or a different one altogether. She's rushing towards me. "What is it?" I say, and she stops.

"There's something out there." She's a little breathless.

"What sort of something?"

"A ghost," she says. "All white and misty and moving quickly between the trees."

"There can't be a ghost," I say, but she's not really listening to me any more. Her fear has propelled her past me and she rushes off towards the buildings.

I do not believe in ghosts. It's more likely that the foolish girl spotted another Land Army girl skulking through the woods. They seem distressingly nocturnal, these girls. Just to set my mind at rest, I continue along the length of this wall, out to the place where the trees begin, and I stand very still, peering into the darkness. Nothing. No movement. No sound. No ghost, I think, and turn back for the quadrangle, satisfied in my belief that there is only this world and nothing beyond it. But I have never been more wrong.

The next morning I walk back over the cobblestones, under the arch, and onto the driveway that leads up the hill to the big house. I am relieved that the house is further away than I'd thought. It is at least a mile distant and I am glad it takes me so long to reach the circular drive. Even with Doris's shortcut, the girls couldn't be dashing up here every five minutes, as I had feared they might do. I remember last night and reprimand myself for wishful thinking.

The house is large and made of grey stone. It looks to be eighteenth century, with its strict proportions—three generous windows each side of the front door and the upper-storey windows aligned with these. Three dormers in the roof, and the house flanked by two enormous chimneys.

Framing the massive front door are a pair of concrete urns. Nothing is growing in them, and a soldier leans up against the left-hand one. He has his eyes shut.

"Excuse me," I say, and he opens his eyes but doesn't get up. He probably thinks I'm a local woman, sent to clean the house. I bristle at this, and I don't like the way he looks at me.

"I'm here to see your CO," I say, with all the imperiousness I can muster. "Would you be so kind as to inform him that Gwen Davis of the Royal Horticultural Society is here."

The soldier is not impressed. "He's in the drawing-room," he says. "Go on, then."

"I have no idea where the drawing-room is."

The soldier sighs and rises slowly to his feet. "All right, ma'am," he says.

The house is infinitely grander than our quarters. Crystal chandeliers. Polished mahogany. Passing the dining room I can see a sideboard gleaming with silver serving dishes. Our food last night was served on chipped plates. Our silverware is tarnished. Amid the stately features of the house, evidence of its new inhabitants. A row of heavy boots in the foyer. A rucksack on the piano bench.

I follow my reluctant guide to the back of the house, to a drawing-room that overlooks the garden. Standing there in front of a gramophone playing what sounds like Mozart is the handsome man from the train station who gave me a ride to Mosel.

"Captain Raley, ma'am," says the soldier, and he disappears back up the hall.

"You?" I say. "You're the CO?"

As the man turns to me, he lifts the needle from the spinning record. "Hum that," he says.

"What?"

"Hum what you just heard." He looks at me intently and I warble over what I think were the last few bars of the piece. "God," he says, stepping away from the gramophone as though bitten. "That was truly awful."

"Well, I didn't come up here to hum," I say, working myself back up into a huff.

"No, of course not." Raley steps up to the gramophone. He places the needle carefully on the record and the music moves into the space between us. We don't speak. Then he lifts the needle again and the music disappears. "Mozart," he says. "The *Requiem*, even. But gone nonetheless. Completely gone. The air is not altered by it. Music is not rain, as the poets insist, because when it rains you can tell that it's rained. With music, there's nothing to show accurately that it was even here."

"There's us," I say. I clear my throat, but I'm not brave enough to attempt humming again.

Raley looks at me. "It's temporary," he says. "The effect on us." He turns the knob on the gramophone and the record stops spinning.

"Well, aren't we temporary also?" I say. I realize, after I've said this, that it is not the right sort of thing to say to a man waiting to be posted into the war. His face suddenly looks all hollow and sad. "Sorry," I say. "I'm always saying the wrong thing. I've spent too long working alone in a laboratory."

"Doing what?"

I think of the neatly labelled row of gangrenous parsnips. "Don't ask," I say. "It wasn't good."

Raley moves away from the gramophone, and the light from the French doors behind him rests on his head and makes him look otherwordly. "Would you like some tea?" he says, and I follow him into the kitchen.

He heats the kettle on the stove, makes the tea, and we sit down on opposite sides of the big kitchen table. The early-morning sun makes a bright pattern on the surface of the wood. I have come up here before the Land Girls were out of bed, dressing in my new clothes, sneaking out undetected. "I have come here to see you," I say, "because it appears my girls have been spending time with your men." Understatement, I think, remembering last night.

"Your girls?" Raley smiles at me. "You? You're the CO?"

I couldn't feel less in command, but I did accept the weight of responsibility. Volunteered, I think bitterly. I volunteered for it. "For lack of a better term, I'm the CO." The sun is heating up my green jersey and making me feel itchy.

"I see," says Raley. "You think our two groups of soldiers should stop fraternizing with one another?"

"Yes. We all have our work to do. We should just get on with doing it."

"But we are waiting to begin our work." Raley leans across the table towards me, his face suddenly serious. "And the beginning of our work could essentially mean the end of our selves. Is it reasonable to expect such restraint from men faced with death?"

I can see how cruel it is to wait here in this beautiful grand house, on this gorgeous estate, to wait here to be sent into the war. The contrast will be so extreme. Better to have waited in a roadside shack or a makeshift shelter in the woods. "Is the waiting unbearable?" I ask.

"Yes," says Raley. "And no, considering the alternative." He settles back in his chair, a skitter of worry across his handsome face. If he were a flower, he would be something magnificent. A giant indigo-blue delphinium. A flower that knows, and practises, how to be in love with itself.

"You know how it is, Commander Davis," he says. "What is outlawed becomes desirable. Forbidden fruit and all that."

I have a sudden and terrifying image of a smiling, naked Roy Peake, arms outstretched, and sitting in the palm of each hand a perfect specimen of his Unknown Pear.

"What about a regular, organized event like a dance?" continues Raley. "Say, once a week, here at the house?"

I don't say anything for a moment or two, let him think I'm giving it my deepest consideration, but I have been swayed to sympathy by his mention of death, and by the sight of him in the drawing-room with the sun tangled in his hair. War, too, is order and chaos. But the actuality of the war itself is only chaos. "Every two weeks," I say. "And we can alternate the location. We have a large dining hall which would be quite suitable for dancing." At least I'll be able to keep an eye on the girls at an organized event. It won't be as easy for them to sneak off with the soldiers.

"Yes, that's right. I had a good look around down there before you all arrived." Raley puts both his hands around his tea mug, looks into it. "In fact, I almost set fire to the place. Lay down in one of the rooms with some candles burning. I woke up and the timbered arch above my head was on fire. A long, shivering halo of flame. I barely got it out with the blankets."

"I know that room. That's my room."

"Is it?" Raley looks up at me in surprise. "Well, fancy that."

Last night I couldn't get to sleep for a very long time. I lay there in the dark, making up letters to Mrs. Woolf, and all the time smelling the fiery char of the room. At one point it was all I could think of. I lay there and imagined myself as the smoke, brushed invisibly onto every surface of the room. Even words and thoughts must be coated in it.

Raley gets up to fetch us more tea. "Do you want to know something funny?" he says. He's pouring out the tea, his back to me. The muscles in his forearm are thick and ropy as a tree root.

"What?" I say.

He hands me my refilled mug of tea, doesn't sit down at the table, but stands beside me instead. I can't see his face unless I look up. His voice sounds very far away, as if he's in a different place from me altogether. "When I was lying in that room, sleeping, and the candles were setting fire to the wood above my head, I was dreaming, such a clear and vivid dream."

"What of?"

"Roses." Raley moves away from me, towards the window. I can't see him at all now. "I was dreaming of a great tangle of roses, and when I woke, the first thing I saw was roses. That wooden arch above my head was a bower entwined with roses. A mass of roses. All on fire."

10

Ever since Jane made that remark at dinner about the Land Girls being akin to potatoes, this is how I have thought of them. I can't be bothered to learn their real names, but I have given each of them the name of a potato. Doris, I have rather unkindly called "The Lumper." The girl with reddish hair I have nicknamed "Golden Wonder." The two who seem the least amenable, and who have potential for disobedience, I have named "British Queen" and "May Queen." The black-haired girl is "Vittelette Noir" ("Vittelette" for short). The one who seems the most unhappy, has a constant downcast expression, has been called "Salad Blue." I have given her the name of what is perhaps the most interesting of all the potatoes, in that it retains its entirely blue flesh even when cooked.

Jane has remained Jane. She seems well apart from the potatoes, both in body and in spirit.

I have rushed back from my meeting with Raley to find the Potatoes waiting for me inside the walled garden. No one looks overjoyed to see me. "Right!" I say, with as much enthusiasm as I can summon. "Glad to see you're all eager and ready to go." No one looks eager. "Potatoes," I say, and almost laugh. "That's what we're here for." I look out at the weedy, untidy vegetable garden. This is where we'll have to start. I need to survey the whole estate and look for other suitable places to grow potatoes, but for now it's best to begin where vegetables have previously been grown, in this kitchen garden. "Weeding and hoeing. Cleaning this mess up ready for seeding," I say. "Organize them," I say to the Lumper, who's standing beside me. "I'll be back in a bit to check on your progress." I stomp off in my over-large wellington boots. As I go through the garden gate I hear Doris say in a quavery voice, "Do any of you feel like weeding?"

I find Jane in the barn just off the main quadrangle. She's mucking out the cows. "I want to buy some chickens," I say. "Where's the money?"

"God, Gwen." Jane visibly jumps at my request. "Don't sneak up on me like that. I almost stabbed myself in the foot." She leans on her pitchfork. "What did you say?"

"Chickens. I want some. There's a run in the garden. We can have our own supply of eggs—rationing be damned—and they can eat the garden waste. A very economical solution all round." I am pleased with my sudden decision.

Jane lights a cigarette. "They warned me about chickens," she says.

"Who?"

"The people who own this place. When they were leaving the instructions for the animals' care. Don't be getting any chickens, now—that's what they said."

"Why ever not?"

"There's a ghost that takes them."

"A ghost? What would a ghost want with a chicken?"

Jane grins at me. "You get so indignant," she says. "I'm just telling you what was told to me."

"But you can't believe it? Ghosts?" I remember the girl, who I've since decided was Golden Wonder, rushing at me through the darkness last night, convinced she'd seen a ghost.

"No, I don't believe in ghosts, even though I've known a worthy candidate." Jane puts a hand on the flank of the cow nearest to her.

"And aren't ghosts meant to be spirits? How can a spirit get hungry? Why choose chicken?" I can't get my mind around the concept of a chicken-thieving poltergeist, but I can see that Jane is no longer really listening to me. "Where's the money?" I say again. "And should you be smoking in here?"

"I know it's called the Women's Land Army," says Jane. "But it's not really an army, you know. We all volunteered, or were volunteered, to be here."

"What do you mean?"

"You're acting like a sergeant major."

What I can get away with in dealing with the Potatoes obviously won't wash with Jane. She is not the least bit afraid of me. This cheers me. "I'm just a bit fired up about the chickens," I say.

"Yes, I can see that. Come on, then." Jane grinds her cigarette out under her heel, leads me past the row of cows to the end of the barn. We stand in front of the two horse stalls. "Older workhorse," says Jane, pointing to the massive beast on the left. "But this boy—" She reaches over the right-hand stall door and the black horse nuzzles against her hand. "This boy knows how to run. He was made for it."

Even though he is partially obscured by the stall door, I can see that the horse is a magnificent creature. "What's his name?"

"Don't know." Jane unlatches the door and slips into the stall. The horse buries his nose in her hair and she reaches up to stroke the side of his face. They seem very familiar with each other. "They probably have names." Jane is now down on her hands and knees at the back of the stall. "But I don't know what they are, and I don't want to confuse them by giving them new, temporary names." She comes back to me, brushing straw from her clothes and carrying a metal box. "This is the money for the care of the animals. I suppose chickens would come out of this lot. The Land Army coffers are in a box I've hidden in the laundry room. Under the mangle. I suppose the money for the potatoes would come out of that lot." She hands the box over to me. "I didn't tell the others," she says. "It's the sort of thing that can cause trouble."

"Quite right," I say. I am anxious to make up for my earlier bossiness. "We'll keep it to ourselves, shall we?"

"Just you, me, and him." Jane leans back against the black horse. She looks so small, resting against his shoulder. "I liked what you said, Gwen," she says. "Last night. About love and solace. About waiting. I've been thinking about it this morning." She looks over the stall door at me, in that clear way I'm almost used to now.

I feel a bit embarrassed about what I said last night to Jane. I don't usually confide in people. In fact, I usually don't even like most people. But perhaps some of why I don't like people is that I think they don't like me.

"Can I ask you something?" I say.

"Of course."

"What do you think . . ." I almost can't say the words. I have to swallow and start again. "My looks," I say. But I can't go on with it. I stop there. I feel shaky, have to rest against the rough wooden door for support.

Jane's features soften. I can't read the emotion. Pity? Sorrow? Sympathy? "Oh, Gwen," she says. "You're not half as bad as you think you are." She reaches into her jumper for another cigarette. "I spent most of February in the hospital ward, watching my cousin die. He was essentially blown apart, although he took a long time to actually die. Just lay there screaming. *Écorcher*, isn't that what they used to call being flayed alive? Colin's skin was peeled back in places, like he was a laboratory specimen. I could see right into him. Do you know what we are, Gwen?" Jane lights her cigarette. Her hands jump as she moves match to tobacco. "We are a mass of purple worms. Veins. Intestines. A mass of twitching, stinking worms. That's why he was screaming, because he could see that for himself. He could see what he was made of, what was there inside him."

"Jane," I say, because she's crying now and I don't know what to do. "Jane."

She leans against the horse, and he lets her. I clutch the metal cash box. I think of the word the doctors had used for Jane's grief. *Distress.* What exactly was that word meant to include?

Grief moves us like love. Grief is love, I suppose. Love as a backwards glance.

After a few moments Jane dries her eyes on her sleeve, turns to me. "Really, Gwen," she says. Her voice is hard and closed now. "You have no idea what beauty is."

11

When I get back to the walled garden there's no one there but the Lumper. The beds are still covered in a tangle of debris. There are several hoes lying haphazardly on the path through the centre of the garden, as though the people attached to them have suddenly evaporated.

"What happened?" I ask the Lumper, who's sitting on a bench in the sun. "Where is everyone?"

"They left."

"Left?"

The Lumper shifts a little uncomfortably on the bench. "They didn't feel like weeding, ma'am."

"It's not a question of what they *feel* like." I can't believe such downright cheek. "Why didn't you stop them?"

The Lumper looks at me blankly. "How?" she says.

"But I left you in charge."

"Well, I did stay behind to report to you."

"Well, that's not good enough, Doris."

The Lumper looks at me blankly again. "Isn't it?" she says. From anyone else this comment would carry the sting of sarcasm, but from her it is full of a kind of fumbling confusion.

"Where did they go?"

"Probably up to the house, ma'am."

"Right." I turn and start to leave the garden. "You wait here. Don't go anywhere. Do you understand?"

"Yes, ma'am." The Lumper kicks out with one of her feet, like a petulant child who hasn't been invited to a party. "But it's not fair if I'm to do all the weeding."

I'm almost at the door to the garden. "I don't care what you do," I shout back, over my shoulder. "Just don't leave." I march across the quadrangle, take the stairs two at a time up to my room, and have to pause for breath on the landing. I march into my room, retrieve the crumpled letter sent by the WLA head office from the floor, and start on my journey to the estate house, for the second time in one day.

This has all become like some terrible grown-up version of boarding school, I think, as I march up the hill. That same sense of being apart from the others. That same feeling of being punished for that exclusion.

Captain Raley is standing by the window in the drawing-room. He seems to have been standing there for quite some time. There's no sign of anyone else about.

"Where are they?" I say.

"Choosing a site for a picnic," he says, without turning around.

"Why didn't you stop them?"

"It's a nice day for a picnic," Raley says. "I didn't feel like stopping them." He does turn from the window now, turns to face me, and I see how tired he looks. "I don't really know these men," he says. "We've only been together a short while. They're leftovers, extras from other regiments. We're being assembled here into a new regiment, and then we'll be shipped out. But we're a disparate group." He gives me a small smile. "Why not have a picnic?" he says.

"Because there's work to be done. Your men might have nothing to do, but my girls are meant to be seeding potatoes."

"You're just annoyed because you've lost control of them," says Raley.

He's right. "I never had control of them," I say. "That's the problem." I look around the room and don't see what I need. "Do you have a telephone up here?" I ask. "I can't find one down where we are."

"In the hall." Raley waves his arm in the direction I've come from, and I walk back out, unrolling the crumpled letter as I go.

I call the local WLA office, and when I get the county rep on the line and am just about to launch into my complaint of the girls, she practically yells down the phone. "Gwen Davis! What happened to you? You were meant to have arrived a week ago. I was just about to send out a replacement for you."

"Well, there's no need," I say. "I just got a little mixed up about the arrival date, but I'm here now."

"We can't have this sort of thing," says Mrs. Billings. "We are an organization that prides itself on efficiency."

"Well," I say, ready again to deliver my speech about the girls.

"I hope you will demonstrate proper conduct from now on ."

"All right," I say.

"I'll be up to see you at the earliest convenience," Mrs. Billings continues.

To check up on me, I think. "All right," I say again,

and replace the receiver to avoid any further lecturing.

"May I suggest a solution?" Raley is standing behind me, startles me with his nearness.

"Please," I say. My hand is still on the phone. I feel near to tears.

"Offer them something," says Raley. "The dance. An outing. Give them what they want and they'll be more co-operative."

"But how do I know what they want?" I am thinking now that I much prefer parsnips to people. They are infinitely more reliable. The stupidity of vegetables is preferable to the unpredictability of people.

Raley touches my arm and my hand lifts from the phone as though pulled up by an invisible wire. "They want a picnic," he says. "Act like you gave it to them."

Doris is still sitting on the bench exactly where I had left her when I walked out of the walled garden. She is tapping her shoes with a stick and humming something unrecognizable. I look around the garden. It is such a mess. "Come on," I say to Doris. "I want you to help me with something."

The Lumper stops humming, looks at me in that blank way of hers that I have difficulty reading. "All right," she says, and lumbers off the bench.

I enlist the Lumper to help me break into the small shed in the walled garden. We pry open the rusted lock with the steel tines of a pitchfork. I had expected the small brick building to be nothing more than a tool shed. In fact, there are no tools in it at all. What is there is far more useful than tools.

The door has settled down on the frame, so the Lumper has to use her rather impressive brute strength to shift it open enough for us to squeeze into the interior. The floor is carpeted in mouse droppings. Along one wall, beneath the only window, is a desk, its pigeonholes having become nests and depositories for the rodents who have lived here most recently. There are still bits of paper resting in some of the slots above the writing surface. A chair is pushed up neatly to the desk, as though someone had just popped out to get a cup of tea and was expected to come right back. The walls are sprouting nails. On one nail hangs what's left of an old pair of gardening gloves. On another nail there's a chewed bit of paper, one word still visible in faded ink—*Sweet.* Sweet peas, I think. Sweet William.

"Do you know what this is?" I say to the Lumper, who's cuffing cobwebs out of her curly hair. "This is the head gardener's office."

"Is it?" she says with complete indifference.

I pull out the chair and sit carefully down at the desk. The wooden surface is patchy with mould. What must once have been a blotter is now a dissolved map of green and brown, stuck quite firmly to the oak desktop. The building must have a leaky roof. "You can go if you want," I say to the Lumper, who's breathing noisily behind me. I hear her inhale loudly as she squeezes through the margin of door and door frame on her way out.

Sitting at the desk I can see the brick wall at the end of the garden opposite, through the filthy, cracked window. The tips of the trees beyond the wall. If I crane my neck, I can make out the roof of the chicken coop.

I don't want to touch the top of the desk, keep my hands curled together in my lap. I look down at them, and at the desk drawer that lies snugly closed just above them. The single, brass handle that fits my right hand perfectly.

What I find in that desk drawer, unharmed by creatures or weather, is the head gardener's ledger.

I take the book outside and sit on a bench in the sun, against the warmth of the brick wall, the gardener's journal open on my knees.

The ledger is a week-by-week job allocation for the estate garden. Everything is marked down in meticulous handwriting on double-page spreads. The book covers the years from 1914 to 1916. At the beginning of the volume, on the opening page, is a list of the twenty-five men who were employed to work in the gardens. Twenty-five men. I look around at the kitchen garden. If I had willing workers, it could be put to rights in a little over a week. What an incredibly busy, productive place this must once have been. I read some of the jobs the men were required to do. *Clip the yews. Train the apples to the wall.* There were North and South gardens. An orchard. There was a lavish mixed border around the quadrangle. There were plans for a water garden on a lower lawn that is now disappeared. I turn to the end of the book. Blank pages. I flip back from there until I find the last entry, written in September of 1916. The last entry, like the first entry, is a list of names. The same names, only the later list has many of the names crossed out. A name with a neat line drawn by a ruler through the middle of it, like a river cleaving its banks. In small lettering beside the names, the word *Killed.* There are only six of the original twenty-five names that have not been crossed out. At the bottom is one sloppily handwritten line. *We will now keep only to the kitchen garden.*

The sun is warm on the page, warm on my skin. I put my hand on top of that list of men and trace their names with a finger. All those gardeners gone off to war. When I was in gardening college I heard someone remark that the only reason such a fuss was being made about training women to be gardeners was that half of Britain's male gardeners had been killed in the Great War. And there was no real recovery from that slaughter. Estates such as Mosel were greatly diminished after that. Probably the kitchen garden was worked and a sort of general overall maintenance was in operation for the duration of the war itself. Then perhaps the estate changed hands and the new owner was primarily interested in the fields, in a high-yield agricultural production, did not want to keep a gardening staff employed. It is very easy to return nature to itself. The clean lines of a garden go first. Then the balance of what has been planted. What used to be a conversation between the different elements becomes a tuneless cacophony. No one thing distinguishable from another.

I spend the afternoon walking purposefully over the estate, the gardening ledger tucked under an arm. I find the North Garden behind the barn. It once must have been a flower garden, perhaps even a market garden. I can find evidence of dahlias, but little else. The garden has, obviously for years now, been used to graze animals, and it is essentially ruined. The same is not true of the South Garden, which lies under bits of broken trees, well behind the dining hall and kitchen garden. The South Garden had been envisaged as a wild garden.

It was planted with bulbs and flowering trees. A meadow garden. Daffodils still brighten the ground, flashes of yellow from the sea of long grass. Beyond the South Garden the farm fields fall away in green shelves. This garden was the exit from the estate, just as the North Garden was the entry to it. This place was the transition between the order of the estate and the order of the natural world. Step away from this garden and you walked down through fields of tall grass, and then into the pleated furrows.

The North Garden would have been more formal. It would have been the first glimpse of a Mosel garden seen through the trees on the drive up to the house. There would have been flowers in rows, tall flowers to be moved by the wind and seen as a woozy sway of colour through the trees as the horse and carriage clattered past.

It occurs to me, standing here now, that I didn't see much in the way of gardens when I was up to visit Raley at the big house. The usual shrubs to define the walkway to the front door, but nothing elaborate in front of the house. It is true I didn't have time to poke around in the back, but I am struck now by the lushness and variety of the gardens here, and the scarcity of ornamental vegetation at the house, where it would seem to be required more. But perhaps the buildings where we are housed predate the house? Certainly the quadrangle is an old design, dating from the Middle Ages. Perhaps this fleet of gardeners were being loyal to a much earlier time than their own when they designed and tended these gardens. And perhaps they didn't design them at all, but merely maintained or rescued what had already been here.

I stand in the middle of the ruined meadow garden. Soon the fruit trees here will be foaming with blossom. There are wild violets in the woods, and pools of bluebells at my feet. It would have been just like leaving land, to leave this garden, to kick through the warm shallows here—flowers breaking like spray above my boots—and step out into the deep, flat ocean beyond. The smell of blossom in my hair like wind.

Whoever made these gardens originally, and whoever kept them going, reinvented them, knew what they were doing. And more than that, I think, looking over the ripple of fields past this meadow—more than that, someone loved this place.

The orchard is to the east, down the slope behind the stables, down the hill from the North Garden, in a small clearing, protected on one side by an old stone wall. Perhaps the wall once enclosed the whole area. There are a few limbs down, but generally the trees are in good shape. Mature trees. Apple and pear. Several have been trained to grow along the wall, their limbs fastened to the stone, made to grow in straight lines so that the fruit will grow evenly. I remember the notation from the book I carry under my arm. *Train the apples to the wall.* Espalier. That's what this method of producing fruit is called. Some consider it artistically pleasing, but I've always found the splayed posture of the crucified tree very unsettling. All its movement is controlled and directed. The tree ceases to be itself and becomes merely the product of an entirely human desire.

The trees espaliered to this wall have been untended

for years. Whereas the branches start firmly attached to the wall close to the trunk of the individual tree, they soon are free to move upwards, move out from the wall. It is as though the bodies of the trees are pinned to the wall and the limbs are reaching out for freedom.

I step around behind the wall, to get away from the sight of the apple trees. There's a path behind the wall. Directly opposite the wall, mirroring it, are a row of huge yew trees, jammed close together from years of never being trimmed so that they form a large hedge, a slumbering green whale.

There's a flash of white under the hedge and I bend down to examine the flower there. An anemone of some sort. I bend closer over the small white flower with the yellow centre. It's strange that I don't recognize it. I am usually quite good with flowers.

The flower is not alone. It is not growing under the yew, but has moved in that direction from where it starts in a small clearing. When I get down on my hands and knees and peer under the hedge I can see a whole river of anemones. I use the gardener's ledger as a shield and push through the hedge. Yew branches feather against my scalp. I breathe in the spicy smell and then I'm past it, standing on top of the river of white anemones and looking at the most unruly garden I have ever seen.

The anemones lead to a huge, overgrown flower bed. Near one end there is some kind of structure, completely choked with greenery. The bed itself is covered with hundreds of nettles. The flowers bloom amid the dead wood and the vegetation of those still dormant or long since dead. I follow the flow of anemones up to the edge of the flower bed. There is not much light here. One side of this garden is flanked by the massive yews. The other three sides are bordered by woods. Some of the trees have woven their branches together over this patch of ground, effectively blocking the sun.

I crouch beside the edge of the garden. I feel something that at first I'm sure is fear. But no, that's not it. What I feel is a kind of unreality. I am a ghost. I have wandered back in time, or forward, and I have disturbed this sleeping place with my presence. The one thing I can clearly feel, the one thing I know above all else, is that I am the first person to have been here in a very long time.

I scrape around in the bed beside the anemones and promptly get stung by the cloud of nettles that has settled over the garden. I poke around in the dirt instead, rubbing it between my fingers to assess its measure. My fingers brush against something solid resting in the earth. Flat stone. A cut rectangle of stone. I rub my fingers along it and feel the indentations open under them like windows. There's something carved into the stone.

It is a word. Not a name as I had presumed. I brush the earth carefully away from the stone with my jersey sleeve. There's a word cut into the slate by a steady hand. A word buried and recovered, as this word always must be, because that is how it works in us, that is how it is read.

Longing.

12

The anemone is an *Anemone narcissiflora.* I look it up in the reference books I have lugged down from London. I barely have time before supper, scrabbling through the pages with grubby hands. I have brought a sample back with me from the garden, although it's a little soiled from having been jammed into my trouser pocket.

The *Anemone narcissiflora* is an alpine flower that grows in meadows in the Pyrenees, the Alps, parts of Spain and Turkey, even in mountains across Siberia to the northern part of Japan. It is a strange thing to find in an English garden.

There are noises in the hall outside my bedroom. The girls are back and on their way to dinner. I snap my book shut, jump up to wash my filthy hands. I have missed lunch today, with all the turmoil and my explorations, and I am famished.

A rigid order in dinner seating arrangements seems to have been established and is being avidly maintained by the group. I take my regular, and now obviously permanent, seat next to Jane. Again, I am the last one to the table. The others glare at me.

"Have you been out climbing trees, Gwen?" Jane whispers to me. She reaches up and pulls bits of yew from my hair, laying them carefully beside my plate as a sort of table decoration.

The doors open and Mabel and Irene enter with bowls of a lumpy pulp that looks very much like the animal swill of last night's dinner. "Rabbit stew," says Irene helpfully, as she puts my dish down in front of me.

I think of the rabbit found in London at the end of January, after a particularly heavy period of bombing. It was running around and around Piccadilly Circus. This wild creature in the midst of ruined London was a miracle for a day, until the rabbit was discovered to be an escaped regimental mascot.

As soon as the village women leave, Jane pushes her bowl away from her.

"Not hungry?" I ask.

"Just doing my bit for food rationing. There's a war on, you know," says Jane.

I can't blame her. The stew is completely tasteless, but I bolt mine down because I am so hungry. Some of the other girls eat only a few spoonfuls before pushing their bowls away as well. No one speaks. I look round at the table of girls, at the bowls of liquefied rabbit, at the huge flag of black unfurled against the windows. It feels as if night itself has entered this room.

No one seems inclined to explain their absence from work today. "I need you to do what you're here to do," I say, but this elicits no response from the girls. I think of what Raley said to me at the house. "Was it a good picnic?" I ask.

Golden Wonder snaps her head up, looks at me warily. Still no one speaks.

"Captain Raley and I will organize dances for you and the soldiers," I say, "but I need you to work in the garden. It's why you're here."

Jane looks over the assembled girls. "That's a fair deal," she says quietly, and the others nod and mumble their agreement. I can't believe how easily she has controlled them. I know I should be thankful, but I immediately feel jealous of Jane's easy authority.

"I'm going to buy chickens," I blurt out. "We can have our own eggs."

Silence. Finally one of them speaks. Vittelette Noir leans on her arms over the table and looks down towards me. At first I think she is talking to me, but as soon as she starts to speak I realize she is talking to Jane. "You know," she says, "I can do better than this."

"What can you do?" says Jane.

"My father owns a hotel in London. I used to work for him in the kitchen." Vittelette Noir looks at the row of Land Girls. "Cooking," she says. There is a murmur of excitement from the others. My mention of chickens garnered no response at all.

"Well," I say. "That will be of no use here."

"Why not?" Jane turns to me, her unflinching gaze doing its usual work to disarm me. I think I prefer it when people glance away from me, disregard me. "Gwen," says Jane, "why couldn't we do our own cooking? Or rather, Elspeth could do our cooking. That's what you're suggesting, isn't it?" she says to Vittelette Noir.

"Yes." Vittelette Noir now addresses her words to me. "Once we all start working in the garden," she says, "I could be spared to work in the kitchen."

"But I've found more ground for the potatoes," I say in protest.

"We could get our ration books back from the village women and you could do the necessary shopping," says British Queen to Vittelette Noir.

"Gwen," says Jane quietly. "How is this different from your chickens? This is just another instance of us taking control of our well-being."

Fine, I think. Mention the chickens now. No one cared about them when I mentioned them. "Do what you have to do," I say to Jane. I don't look at her, keep my head down over my empty bowl. I get tangled up, trying to get on with these girls. If I order them about, try to keep them organized, then I'm being too bossy. If I try to be nice to them, they ignore me or regard me with complete suspicion. They have enjoyed days here without me, and have probably formed a united front against me. I stand up, abruptly knocking the table with my knee. The dishes jiggle.

"Where are you going?" asks Jane.

"I don't know." I feel very close to tears. "I was happy about the chickens," I say too loudly, causing several of the others to look in my direction. British Queen shakes her head sadly at May Queen.

"Gwen, sit down. Please." Jane tugs at my arm. "Think how happy you'll be when Elspeth makes you a lovely omelette out of those eggs from your chickens. Please." She tugs at my arm again and I fall back into my chair like a chastened child.

I still feel like crying. Nothing is going well. No one ever likes me. I'm not good with people. I've been too isolated most of my life. I don't know how to get on with others. Why did I ever think that volunteering for this job was a good idea?

"Look," says Jane. "You've still got tree in your hair." She reaches up and gently removes the pieces of yew. This makes me feel even more like a child. No, worse than that, like some silly, helpless pet. But I let her do it. I feel alternately that I am vastly superior to her and that I am not worthy of her attention at all.

After supper the girls leave for one of the downstairs rooms in the west wing. A wireless has been discovered there by Golden Wonder and they're off to listen to the nightly war broadcast. I have a dim recollection of a time when the evening broadcast was news of the world. Now it is solely news of the war. What places have been hit by the German bombs. What lies in ruins or burns to ashes.

I go into the kitchen to do the washing-up from supper. It is an excuse not to have to join the group. It is also something of a plea for sympathy. I don't know how to make them like me. This is all I can think of at the moment. If they've failed to be impressed by the dance and the chickens, I don't have much else at my disposal.

Jane has gone off to tell Mabel and Irene that we will no longer be needing them to cook for us. She comes back while I'm washing up, hops onto the kitchen worktop beside the sink, and lights a cigarette. "Done," she says cheerfully. She unfolds a fan of ration books and waves them in front of my face. "Our destiny is in our hands."

"It's not just the cooking," I say, not prepared to let go of my reservations without a bit of a fight. "She'll have to keep the range and boiler going. There's hot water and—"

"There's a whole cellar full of coal," Jane says, cutting me off. "She's done this before. That's the important thing. This is what she knows how to do. What she wants to do." Jane flicks her cigarette ash into my sink full of soapy water. "Omelette," she says. "Soufflé. Victoria sponge with cream and jam."

I have to smile. "Why do you bother with me?" I say. "I'm not like the others."

"Precisely. You're infinitely more interesting than the others. You're complicated. They are young and barely formed. They only want to please or be pleased. But you—" Jane stabs her cigarette towards my face for emphasis. "You aren't as easily defined as that."

I stop washing the dishes, my hands up to the wrists in soapy water. But I am easily defined, I think. *Longing.* The word I found today comes back with such force I sway against the sink. I almost tell Jane about that garden. I actually open my mouth to tell her, and then I shut it again. What would I tell her? What would I say? I don't really know what to make of it myself. Then I realize what I felt when I found that garden this afternoon. That I was the first person to see it aside from the person or people who made it. And that it was meant for me and me alone to find. I do not want to share it with anyone, even Jane.

"What?" says Jane. She has been watching me, can tell I was on the verge of speaking.

"Were you close to your cousin?" I lift a heavy plate from the warm water and heft it into the dish rack. It is all

I can think of to say. When all else fails, ask a question.

"When Colin and I were small," says Jane, "we were very close. Constant companions. Inseparable. All that rot you've ever read about a close family, that was us." She swings down off the worktop, grabs a towel from the handle of the range, and starts to dry the dishes from the rack.

"What happened?" I ask.

"We grew up." Jane opens the cupboard above her head and clatters the dry bowls into it. "This is what I know. I was close to Colin. Then I wasn't. Then, when he was lying in the hospital dying, I was close to him again. The funny thing was that I recognized him in his pain, recognized that little boy from when we were young and the equivalent of in love with each other. It was his screaming that did it. His screaming brought him back to me." Jane leans against the worktop. "And then he left me for good," she says. "In the moment he returned, he left."

I'm afraid she is going to start to cry again, but she doesn't, just stands against the worktop, the damp tea towel slung over her shoulder. "This is what I know," she says again. "Because I was close to Colin when we were young, because I had the example of that, I knew how to love. I knew what intimacy was and I wanted it. Because of Colin, I knew about love."

"And then there was Andrew," I say.

"Yes, Andrew." Jane takes a glass from the rack and wipes it dry. "Andrew is missing. But missing isn't dead."

I think of Mrs. Woolf, and the hasty way her death has been anticipated. "I know," I say. "Missing isn't even lost. It just means someone isn't where they're expected to be."

"Exactly."

"And where is Andrew expected to be?"

"Malta. He was on his way there." Jane abandons the wet tea towel and reaches for a cigarette. "He's RAF," she explains. "He was flying a mission to an aerodrome in Malta and his plane disappeared somewhere over the Mediterranean. But the thing is this—" Jane lights her cigarette. I'm not looking at her, but out of the corner of my eye I can see the jumpy match. Her hands are shaking again. I hear her inhale deeply. "The thing is this, Gwen. No wreckage was found. There were six men in that Wellington. No wreckage. No bodies. And he's ditched before and survived. And the Mediterranean's warm. And he's a good swimmer."

I let the water out of the sink. There's a great sucking sound as it disappears down the drain. "Those are good facts," I say. "Hang on to them."

The last of the water leaves the sink and I see the one small plate lying stranded on the bottom of the porcelain. It was easily missed. I pick it up carefully and put it gently in the rack.

13

I move my bed directly underneath the timbered arch in my room. I lie there, with the weight of *The Genus Rosa* pinning me to the mattress, and I imagine Raley's fiery bower overhead. Longing, I think. *Longing.* Sometimes I think I might die of it.

Jane has had someone to long for, someone to love. She can probably still remember the weight of him on top of her. But maybe that's not true either; maybe the physical presence of someone doesn't stay around after they've gone, doesn't hang in a room like smoke. Maybe longing itself is the ghost, and all evidence of the actual lover vanishes instantly.

The Genus Rosa feels unbearably heavy tonight. I lie on my back and think of Raley's fiery roses above my head. I must ask him what colour they were. I like to know the names of things. Maybe I can figure out what kind of roses appeared to him in that dream he had.

I think of the anemone I found in that neglected garden today. An *Anemone narcissiflora.* Why is that longing? Is it to do with the myth of Narcissus—the boy who fell in love with his own reflection? And then I think of the common name for anemones. Windflower. Anemones are opened by the wind. Yes, I think, that's it. Longing is opened by the wind.

I don't have the blackout curtains pulled yet in my room, but I have no lamp lit, no light to be glimpsed from outside. And besides, here in the depths of Devon there don't seem to be any wardens going around checking for chinks of light between the curtains, as there were in London. Not much danger of the five-pound fine for having a streak of light showing. It is so nice not to have the curtains pulled. I can see the pale cast of moonlight in the sky. If I arch my neck back, I can see a fine spray of stars above the quadrangle.

Anemones are opened by the wind. They are hard to raise from seed, and are not easily divided.

Sometimes *The Genus Rosa* is the exact weight of my loneliness. I push it off me, struggle off the bed, and go over to the window. I shove open the glass and thrust my head out into the cool night air. It's after midnight. There's the smell of damp rising from the stones of the building. Off in the distance there's the soft call of a nightingale. I look down at the strict rectangle of the quadrangle. There's a dark blur, moving from the shadows of this building, running across the grass towards the stables. From this angle and height I can't tell who it is. The moon disappears behind a cloud and I momentarily lose the figure in the shadows of the opposite buildings. When the moon returns, the figure has vanished.

14

In the next week we finally settle into a routine at Mosel. The chickens are purchased and moved into the coop in the walled garden. They are fed kitchen scraps and almost immediately start producing eggs. Even though no one was enthusiastic about the chickens when I first mentioned them, the actual fact of the eggs has cheered everyone up no end.

Vittelette Noir has vastly improved the evening fare. She cooks dishes with names I can't pronounce. She occasionally bakes fresh bread. Sometimes she even manages to cook a pudding to follow the main course. She makes a very good flan. In honour of her new duties in the kitchen, I have secretly renamed her Victualette Noir.

After our initial faulty start there is now a rhythm to our days, a certainty of routine that, I hope, provides some comfort to us all. Jane rises first in the mornings, well before any of the rest of us are even awake, and goes out to milk the cows. Breakfast is porridge and tea, both laced with the fresh milk Jane has procured. Then, after breakfast and washing-up, Jane takes the cows and the two horses out to graze, and the rest of the girls go to work in the walled kitchen garden. They have started planting the potatoes there now, having cleared off all the debris and prepared the ground for the setting of the seed. I have also had them plant cabbage, peas, broad beans, runner beans, and onions, since there is currently an onion shortage in Britain.

Ever since the decision to take control of our own cooking, there has been a mood of self-sufficiency among the girls. There is a marked improvement in their attitude, or perhaps they have just become more adept at their various deceptions. I cannot tell. But I am grateful they have decided, under Jane's prodding, to work the garden. I periodically forget that we are meant to be doing all this agricultural production for the war effort, and have to stop myself thinking that it is just for our own survival. It appears that everyone feels much the same way. *Our food*, we say to one another. *Our potatoes. When our harvest is ready.*

In a day or so, when the kitchen garden is fully planted, the girls are to move on and prepare the South and North gardens for potatoes. After the land is cleared it will have to be ploughed. There is no evidence of a tractor on the property. Perhaps it broke, or was loaned out to a neighbouring farm. But there is an old plough in the barn, and when the time comes, Jane has assured us the horses can be relied upon to pull it.

While the girls are busy in the kitchen garden, I sneak out to work in the hidden garden. In just under a week I have made great progress with it. I have cleared out the insulating layer of nettles that was covering the whole bed, and I have had a good look at what is underneath.

The garden has been purposefully planted. I can tell this immediately from the balance of flowers already in bloom and those that have yet to show themselves. Until I can work out the meaning of everything, I am making my way very methodically up the bed from the anemones I first discovered. I am cutting back plants, trying both to account for natural growth and not slaughter them entirely, and to tidy their shapes so that no one plant is completely dominated by another.

I work most of the day in the hidden garden. I have told no one of this place, pretend to the others that I am roaming the estate looking for suitable planting areas. Sometimes I say I am working in the orchard, since it is on the other side of the wall, and if I am spotted, it will be where I am spotted.

Work stops for the day by five o'clock. In the two hours before dinner the girls have baths or sit outside, talking or writing letters. After dinner it has become customary to gather in the room with the wireless and listen to the nightly broadcast. I think we do this partially to remember that there is a war on and that this is the reason we are here.

Tonight is Saturday night. It is the first dance with the Canadian soldiers up at the house. There is great excitement in the halls after dinner as the girls prepare themselves for the evening. I can hear them rushing in and out of each other's rooms as I stand at the window in mine.

"Aren't you going?" It's Jane, at the door of my bedroom.

"Yes, I'm going."

"But you're still all grubby from crawling through muddy ditches, or whatever it is you do in the day." Jane comes into my room. "It still stinks in here," she says, sitting down on my bed and lighting a cigarette. "The least you could do for all those eager lads is to put on a clean jersey."

"But I'm not good at this sort of thing." I had actually been thinking of not going to the dance at all, until I realized that I needed to make a visit to the estate house and the dance would provide a good cover for my true intentions.

"Not good at what? Dressing? Or life?" Jane flops backwards on my bed and there's a solid thump as her head hits *The Genus Rosa.* I had fallen asleep last night with it in the bed with me and had forgotten to remove it this morning.

"God," says Jane, putting a hand to her head. "What do you have in here? Souvenirs from the garden? A few stones from the field?"

"Sorry," I say, and slide the one volume of *The Genus Rosa* away from her before she can get a good look at it.

"Let me change. I'll meet you downstairs." I don't want to be asked or to have to answer any questions about Miss Willmott's weighty botanical nemesis. "I'll just be a few minutes. Please."

"A few minutes," repeats Jane. She gets up from the bed, still rubbing her head. "Don't change your mind, Gwen. Don't let me suffer that moony pack of puppies alone."

I don't change my mind. I put on a clean jumper, as instructed, and I meet Jane in the quadrangle in exactly ten minutes. The Potatoes have left already, the whole cheery group of them halfway to the house by the time we get out to the driveway. Even in the thickness of the early dark we catch glimpses of them on the road ahead of us. They are like one big, blowzy flower, swaying this way and that, over the road and back again. Each one of them a moving petal in the dark.

By the time Jane and I arrive at the house there's no one left at the front door to greet us. The soldiers must have assumed that the first group of girls was the only group. It suits both Jane and me to let ourselves into the house. We stand together in the hall. From within the house there are the sounds of a gramophone, laughter, the slick tattoo of shoes on a wooden floor. They must have rolled the carpet back in the dining room.

"Right," says Jane, beside me. "I'm going to see about something to drink. You coming?"

"In a minute," I say. "There's something I have to do first."

"You are ever mysterious," says Jane. She starts along the hall. "But I do find it endearing. Come and rescue me when you've completed your mission." She disappears down the long panelled hall into the noisy throng at the end.

I find what I'm looking for on the second floor, at the front of the house. The room is dark. The door is open. I slip inside and gently pull the doors closed behind me, then begin my search at the large oak desk by the window.

"Well, hello." It is Raley. He's sitting in a wing chair by the fire. I am so startled I almost scream. I do jump a little and knock my hand against the desk lamp.

"Captain Raley," I say.

"Captain Davis."

"Why aren't you dancing?"

"I'm not really one for dancing." Raley turns on the lamp beside his chair and we can see one another clearly now. "I came up here to do some reading and I must have fallen asleep." There is a small book on his knees. "I always feel that I'm defending myself before you. Why is that?"

"I think I attack when I'm on the defensive," I say. "Out of nerves."

"You would make a good soldier with those instincts," says Raley. "Why don't you go instead of me. I would be quite happy to dig for potatoes."

I remember what Jane said to me the other day. "It's called the Women's Land Army," I say, "but really it isn't anything like an army at all."

"Except for the uniform." Raley pulls a flask from under his jacket, uncaps it, and drinks. He holds it out to me.

"No, thank you." I have never been much of a drinker. The one time I did imbibe too much, at a Royal

Horticultural function put on by the Narcissus and Tulip Committee, I became very sincere. Too sincere. I sat beside an elderly couple and rhapsodized about spring flowers. I think I might have quoted Wordsworth.

"To your health, then." Raley takes a swallow on my behalf. "What can I do for you, Captain Davis?"

"I'm looking for a plan of the estate. I need to find information about some of the gardens. Have you seen a plan of the estate anywhere?"

"No, I haven't. But you're welcome to search. And you're right, this would be the place to find it." Raley picks up his book. "I'll just sit here and read and keep you company, shall I?"

"If you want," I say. I never know with Captain Raley if he's joking or not. He is very hard to gauge. My first instincts are to not trust him, to treat his politeness and courtesy as suspicious. But I do find him likeable, in spite of myself. And I do respond to his kindness with such appetite that I realize I have been starved for kindness. "I didn't mean to just barge in," I say.

Raley waves his book at me. "Search away," he says. "It really isn't my house either, is it? It's a place we live in for now. That's all."

Like our lives themselves, I want to say, but I don't. He's picked up his book again. I start poking through the drawers of the desk.

There's nothing in the desk. There's nothing on the shelves beside the desk. The books on the walls are in alphabetical order by author and I am confused by this. Would a plan of the estate be on those shelves at all? And under what? *P* for Plan? *E* for Estate? I look under

M for Mosel, but there's nothing there beside William Morris. I move around to search the low shelves on the other side of Raley's chair.

"What are you reading?" I ask.

"Tennyson. That poem he wrote about his friend who died."

"*In Memoriam*?" I bend down to scrabble through the shelves near the floor where there appear to be sheaves of paper stacked up in piles.

"Yes." Raley clears his throat. "'Our little systems have their day;/ They have their day and cease to be.' Isn't that what we are doing here, Gwen? Creating little systems. To pass the time, I sometimes force the men to do a scavenger hunt, or play word games—to stop them creeping down the hill to you, or stabbing their bayonets into trees."

"Aren't you meant to be training?" I ask.

"Training," says Raley derisively. "Marching through the fields with heavy rucksacks on? There'll be time enough for that when we get over there. I'd rather rest the men than tire them out."

The stacks of paper are sheet music for piano. A Bach prelude. A Chopin étude. "Did you have a friend who died?" I ask, still on my hands and knees beside Raley's chair, pawing through the shelves above the sheet music.

Raley reads from the book, his voice rich and slow. "'And thy dark freight, a vanished life,'" he says. "'An awful thought, a life removed,/ The human-hearted man I loved,/ A Spirit, not a breathing voice.'"

That is my answer, then. "The poem sounds better than I remember," I say.

"Yes," agrees Raley. "He says these very lovely things, like: 'He put our lives so far apart/We cannot hear each other speak.' And has vivid images, such as how 'the trees/Laid their dark arms about the field.' But it's all an ascension to God. He can't live with his grief unless he surrenders it to a higher purpose."

I can hear Raley unscrew the top of his flask and drink. "On the shelf right next to *In Memoriam*," he says after a moment, "I found this monograph by a Reverend F. W. Robertson. It's an odd little analysis of Tennyson's poem. Some of his observations are quite touching. Some are so blatantly simple that they seem utterly pointless. Listen. He will say something not bad, like: 'First mood of sorrow. The eternal gloom of the yew tree is felt to be congenial.' And then he will say something clumsy and rather stupid: 'The heart finds relief in metrical expression.' Or, 'The quiet English grave. Funeral feelings.' What exactly is a 'funeral feeling'?"

I think I have found the estate plan. It's in a cardboard tube, labelled on the outside "Plan of the Grounds." I remove the metal cap from one end and begin to extract the roll of paper. "What's the point of it, then?" I say. Raley must be drunk. This is the most talkative he's ever been.

"The point," says Raley slowly. "Captain Davis, you are a trifle pedantic. The point." I can almost hear him thinking beside me as I unroll the paper, confirm that it is indeed a plan of the estate, and drop it back into the tube.

" 'There are truths which are to be proved only by faith and feeling.' That was one of his better observations," says Raley. "The Reverend F. W. Robertson.

The point, dear Davis, is that sometimes what you want is nothing more than to put your name beside someone else's, someone whom you love. Stretch your name out alongside theirs as though it was you, lying next to them."

I stand up. The room is hot and it suddenly seems hard to breathe. Raley is quiet now, beside me. I don't mean to, but I lean over and touch his hair. It is waxy with hair cream. "Come downstairs with me," I say. But he shakes his head no. He has his eyes closed. I gently push a lock of hair away from them, the way my mother once brushed the rain from my forehead. And he lets me. When he speaks again his voice is soft with emotion.

"Poetry is no use," he says. "I thought it might be, but the poetic moment is a static one. It's watching through a window while the action happens elsewhere. And then the poet turns from the window because the poem is done. Or turns to God. Or turns from the poem itself. It cannot unflinchingly stare grief down. At some point, by necessity, or design, it must turn away. How can I remember if I can't keep pace with the loss?" Raley opens his eyes and looks at me. His face is open and vulnerable. I can see now why it is necessary for him to hide behind a veneer of charm and easy manners. At heart he is unprotected, has been growing precariously on a rock face somewhere in a bitter winter wind.

"I need something to keep pace with me," says Raley. "I need something to move as quickly as I am moving away from him."

The fire crackles in the grate like gunshot. I take my hand from Raley's forehead. I don't know what to say to him. While I was intent on finding the map of the estate, pawing through the shelves, he was reading to me. He was *reading* to me. And what can I say about poetry? He's right in what he feels. I have often thought that poetry is a way to name loss, but it cannot accompany one on the journey of loss.

"Come downstairs with me," I say.

It seems louder on the ground floor than when I was there before. The gramophone seems louder. The voices. Laughter. The scuff of shoes on the wooden floor. I stand briefly at the doorway of the dining room, with Raley behind me. "Where's Jane?" I ask British Queen, who's dancing near to me.

"Kitchen," she shouts over the shoulder of her blond dancing partner.

I stand at the doorway for a moment longer, before leading Raley down the hallway. I feel a sudden wash of responsibility. I should be more carefully chaperoning these girls. They are getting out of hand again. But I look at the room of moving bodies. The room is lit with their youth and laughter, with their carefree energy. I cannot say no to a room like that. "Come on," I say to Raley, and we head for the kitchen.

Jane is in the kitchen. She is standing behind a soldier who is seated in a chair. They are in the middle of the room. There is no one else around them. I recognize the soldier from the train station, my first day in Devon. David. That is his name. David from Newfoundland. It occurs to me that I've never asked Raley where he's from. I almost do this now, almost turn to him behind me in the doorway, when I see the scissors in Jane's hand above David's head. She's cutting his hair.

Change the scene and this story could be different. This could be Jane's house, or mine. She could be married to David. Raley and I could be joining them for dinner. The thing with war is this—we cannot change ourselves enough to fit the shape of it. We still want to dance and read. We hang on to a domestic order. Perhaps we hang on to it even more rigorously than before.

David has his eyes closed. His hair is the colour of wheat. Jane's hands move like slow birds over it. I can see how much she wants to land there, how much she wants to touch him. I can feel the heat of Raley behind me, feel his breath in my hair. And I almost lean back. I almost do. But at that moment Jane looks up and sees me standing in the doorway, and the moment is over. She has that dazed, vacant expression that I recognize from when my mother was dying. It's waking up and not knowing where you are.

"Gwen," she says, her hands still raised above David's head, his eyes still closed. "I need to go home."

Outside, Golden Wonder is kissing a soldier on the front step. They don't seem to notice Jane and me at all as we step around them, step off the ledge of stone into the watery dark.

"I didn't know you could cut hair," I say to Jane as we start down the hill.

"It's what I did in that other life," she says. "Remember that other life?"

"Barely." It does seem that each day folds up a little more of that life I used to have.

Jane is quiet beside me. There are the dark blurs of trees on either side of the road. Stars seeding the night sky.

"I have to love him fiercely in absentia," she says finally. "I cannot falter, or he won't come back." She might be crying, but I cannot tell. I shift the tube with the estate plan in it from one arm to the other, and reach out with my free hand until I find hers. I hold on to it for our whole journey down the hill.

"Look," I say. "Look out there, at the night. This night." For maybe this is how poetry can be of use. Though it can't move with us, we can move it between us, pass it among us, so it is held up by our voices, so it moves with our very breath, our living breath. "Look how the 'trees have laid their dark arms about the field.'"

15

I cannot sleep. The night grows huge around me as I sit up, in my room, with the estate plan spread out on my bed. I use *The Genus Rosa* to anchor it securely to the mattress.

The plan is from 1900, and it shows a very detailed rendering of the gardens. The North and South gardens are much as I have imagined them. There are plans for a water garden, and plans for a maze, drawn onto the diagram with dotted lines to show that they exist only on this paper and in someone's imagination. I like this, like that what is there and what is imagined can lie side by side on the same sheet of paper.

The orchard is drawn, with its stone wall. Behind it the row of yews and paved walkway, called, appropriately enough, Yew Walk. But behind the fence of yews nothing is marked on the plan, nothing to indicate the garden I have found. "Woods," it says, for that entire area. Whoever made that garden made it between 1900 and 1916, when the estate was emptied of its gardeners by the war.

I am restless. I pace the room. I lean my head against the wardrobe. For once, even the thought of lying under *The Genus Rosa* does not calm me. I roll up the estate map and slip it back into its sheath. I walk to the window and fling it open.

Mosel seems such a world of its own. It is hard sometimes to imagine or remember another one. But this estate is quite far south in Devon. It must be near the sea, and tonight there is a wind blowing from that direction. I can smell the tang of the sea. The air has a salt fuse. It reminds me of the Thames, of leaning over the Embankment balustrade and smelling the river smoking by, below me in the dark.

Leaning over the sill into the dark above the courtyard, I see again a figure rushing over the quadrangle. The same figure? I think so, but I am too high to tell who it might be. I pull back into the room, race to the door, and hurl myself down the flight of stairs, practically kicking open the door at the bottom.

I stand out on the gravel path beside the grim memory of the mixed border. Nothing. The figure has completely vanished. How could it disappear so quickly? I remember that Land Girl rushing out of the darkness towards me, how shaken she was by what she had convinced herself she'd seen. A ghost. Is that what I have seen? I was quick to scoff at the idea of ghosts with her and Jane, but I have felt something in the garden I discovered. I have felt the presence of something other. And now, standing in the dark, with a salt wind blowing up from the invisible sea, from the remembered beloved river, I don't know what to think. Am I wish? Am I instinct? Has something forgotten suddenly remembered itself. *Longing.* What is longing if not the ghost of memory?

16

My discovered garden is really three gardens. They are joined together, each naturally flowing out of the other. But the other two are not yet in bloom, so it feels wrong to explore them until they have fully revealed themselves.

The person who planted the Garden of Longing was clever. There are no simple, declarative statements in the plantings. No forget-me-nots or bleeding hearts. The message is much more subtle than that, has to be worked at for meaning.

The more time I spend tending this garden, the more aware I am of how deliberately it has been planted. If not grouped by an emotional category, these plants would never be arranged together. To the eye, it is not a pleasing array. But this garden has not been planted for the eye. It has been planted for the heart. And here I think I am instinct. I follow the line of what I feel in relation to what is planted here.

Erysimum semperflorens is native to Morocco. It grows in scrub and rocky places. It grows in dunes by the sea. It has narrow leaves and dense spikes of small four-petalled flowers. It is vigorous and hardy. It flowers almost continuously. *Semperflorens* means ever-flowering.

I trim the sides of two adjoining yews to create a space to squeeze through every day, without risking injury to myself, but making the entrance small enough so that it cannot be seen by anyone who might happen by. The more time I spend in this quiet refuge, the more private and secret it becomes. And the more convinced I am that it was meant for me to find. Jane is the only one of the girls who pays close enough attention to me to wonder about my daily whereabouts, but I cover myself by moving freely about the estate and making sure I'm seen in a variety of places. I only duck into this garden when I am quite sure there is no one else about. And really, it is easy. No one ever seems to venture down as far as the orchard. The girls are more interested in going up the hill, away from our quarters and towards the big house, in the hopes of meeting up with a soldier, than they are in coming down here.

It is a sunny afternoon in late April. I am weeding the Garden of Longing, turning the earth to break up the clods. If you allow it to do so, earth becomes rock.

There is heat on my back, and the muscles in my arm feel stretched and taut; used, they feel used. I had forgotten how good it can feel to grow tired in one's body from using it up. Spent. Down on my knees at the edge of the flower bed with a slight ache in my shoulder and the sun on my skin, I feel spent.

Lathraea clandestina grows in wet woods or in meadows near streams. Seeds lying in the soil are kept moist and germinate easily. It is a leafless plant. Nothing to protect the flowers, which emerge directly from the ground.

17

At the end of the week the kitchen garden has been fully prepared and planted, and we shift our combined attentions to readying the ground of the North Garden. For this, I need the energies of everyone. Even Jane. Even the horses. We spend most of the morning assembling and finding the necessary pieces of equipment for ploughing, hitching the horses up to the traces. No one really knows what they are doing, but everyone has a little piece of information about the procedure, enough information for us to continue with my plan—although, in retrospect, we should never have attempted what we did.

Jane remembers ploughing from her childhood on the farm. But what she remembers is watching it, as a child, which is not much use. British Queen had a boyfriend who was a farmer. What she knows is how to unhitch the horses from their traces and leave the field for the day. I think, How difficult can it be? Victualette

Noir says, "It's only digging," as we stand around inside the barn, contemplating the strips of wood and metal that make up the fact of the plough.

My idea is a simple one. Even though it is not the right time of year to plough the ground, I want to use the plough to turn the earth of the North Garden, to make the ground easier to prepare for a crop of potatoes. A few times up and down the pasture with the horse. The furrows don't even need to be straight. It should be easy.

It takes a great deal of time and effort to get the plough out of the barn. It is much heavier than it looks and has to be lifted rather than dragged, in case we accidentally plough up the neat, flat surface of the quadrangle. It takes most of the morning to haul the plough around the back of the barn to the North Garden. During this time Golden Wonder pulls her shoulder out of alignment, and Salad Blue cuts her finger on a slivered piece of wood. There is a good half an hour lost while we examine and discuss these injuries. Then Jane slips back to the stables to get the horses, while we untangle the traces from where we've dumped them on the ground beside the plough.

"Speed the plough," says Salad Blue darkly. She holds her cut finger straight up in the air, as though she's continuously on the verge of making an important point.

It turns out that only one horse knows how to plough. The old one. The young black one gets all skittish in the traces. The old horse remembers the weight of the plough, and the slow, steady pace required to keep it moving certainly over the ground. The owners of the estate must have started ploughing by tractor in the time between retiring the old horse and acquiring the new one.

It is the Lumper who knows the most about what is required to plough a piece of ground. She takes control of the plough, sets it firmly in the earth, and holds it steady in its slow journey forward. The rest of us bounce along beside her, touching bits of the equipment or the horse, more out of a need to reassure ourselves that we are doing something than out of actual usefulness. But, as we all bump along the ground together, all of us connected to the fragile machine we've barely mastered, all of us connected to each other, there is a feeling of strength among us. I can see the sweat on the Lumper's forehead, and the straining muscle in British Queen's arm as she pushes against the wooden handle of the plough. I can see the thin, bent body of Jane up ahead of us, leading the horse forward. Even Golden Wonder, who is skipping alongside us, clutching her bad shoulder with her good hand, even she is what we all are—equal to this moment, equal in this moment.

And then we reach the end of the small field and realize we haven't left enough room to turn the horse around.

"Oh, bloody hell," says Salad Blue. The horse is right up against the trees that border the driveway. We will have to unhook the traces and manually turn the plough around. There is silence.

I should have known better. I shouldn't have been carried along by my own enthusiasm. Now the girls will blame me for this, be all bad-tempered and unwilling.

Our brief moment of unity will be gone forever. I have done it wrong. I don't know what I'm doing.

"Come on, then," says the Lumper to British Queen. "Help me with this." She is already at work detaching the horse from the plough. British Queen obligingly helps her out. Jane holds the horse steady. No one complains. No one looks at me as though it is all my fault. And even though we are unhitching the plough, I feel so elated by everyone's good humour and co-operation that I just want to keep going. I want the horse to walk through the trees, across the road, over the fields, and down to the sea, a vein of earth opening behind him.

There's the sound of a car on the other side of the row of trees. It approaches slowly from the bottom of the hill, from the direction of the village. I hear it slow as it climbs the hill towards us—slow, and then stop completely.

The plough is free from its harness, and we are all straining under its weight, lifting it from its furrow and turning it to face the opposite direction, when a short, plump woman in a mackintosh suddenly bursts through the row of trees along the driveway. "Girls!" she says, with a certain note of surprise in her voice, as though she could just as easily have stumbled upon some other exotic creature. Giraffes! Dancing penguins!

"Oh, hello," says Jane. She looks over at me. "Mrs. Billings," she says.

The county rep claps her hands, startling the horse, and says, with alarming cheerfulness, "What a perfect morning for cultivation!"

Salad Blue snorts from behind me. "Hello," I say,

stepping forward. "We haven't met. I'm Gwen Davis." I leave out the bit about the Horticultural Society.

"Ah," says Mrs. Billings. "You're from the Horticultural Society." She looks me up and down, as though I am an actual plant specimen. "The one who took so long arriving."

"Yes."

"Well, at least you're here now. Where you belong." Mrs. Billings steps briskly around the horse, looking down at our one wobbly furrow. "I see you are all keeping busy. Good." She looks like some sort of beetle in her shiny mackintosh. "And how are Mrs. Purvis and Mrs. Crane working out?"

"Who?" says Jane. She has moved over, closer to where Salad Blue and I are standing.

"The women from the village who cook for you," says the county rep. She has turned to face the group of us, her little beetle antennae bristling. I feel as though I am back in primary school.

"We got rid of them," I say. "We're doing for ourselves now."

The beetle puts her hands on her hips. "You can't get rid of them," she says.

"Chaperones," Jane whispers in my ear.

"Why not?" I say. "We prefer to do for ourselves."

"But everything must go through me," says Mrs. Beetle.

"Everything probably does go through her," says Jane unkindly, *sotto voce*.

"There are rules," continues the rep. "You don't own this place. You don't live here."

"But we do live here," says the Lumper. She has one

hand on the plough, her face all grimy with sweat. She looks as though she has been working a plough for years.

Is it really possible to think in abstract terms when we are using our bodies so completely? Is it possible to do something "for the war" and not attach it to one's personal life? We are here together at Mosel because of the war. We are doing this work because of the war. But we are doing this work with our selves and so, in a large measure, it cannot help but be about us. The Lumper is right. It is very simple. We do live here.

"Let me show you what we've done," I say, and I lead Mrs. Billings away from the North Garden, towards the newly restored kitchen garden. She follows me rather reluctantly, making small gasps as she walks on her little beetle legs down behind the stables. As I wait for her to catch up, I look back at the girls. They have turned the plough around. Everyone has claimed a position at the machine. Jane guides the horse. They all move forward over the new ground.

That night Victualette Noir cooks us fish with a mustard sauce that is truly delicious. She makes a rice pudding for dessert. We eat and talk with more appetite than usual and later we all go down to the room with the wireless.

London bombing continues unabated. The port of Plymouth is also being heavily hit. The battle of the Atlantic is on and Britain has already lost well over a hundred ships. For some reason the Admiralty has decided to name all the corvettes in the fleet after delicate flowers. It is odd to hear of the *Campanula* under escort from the *Hyacinth* and the *Bluebell*. One of the ships is even called the *Convolvulus*, which, besides being an excellent flower for a rock garden, is a very tricky word. I imagine the radio-man on that corvette trying to get the name of the ship out in a hurry when they are under attack. As a flower, the convolvulus is pretty. As a weapon of war, I fear it might be doomed.

The other news is even more depressing. It is conjectured that Hitler's advance into the Mediterranean is inevitable and perhaps even unstoppable. I look over at Jane, sitting in a chair by the window, her knees drawn up to her chin, arms wrapped tightly around her legs. How does she survive the uncertainty of her fiancé's disappearance?

"I hate those curtains," says Salad Blue suddenly. "They make me feel as though I'm inside a tomb."

"Maybe it's curtains for us," says Jane. But no one laughs.

"Wait," says May Queen. "I've got an idea." She rushes from the room with what, for her, is unusual speed. We can hear her clatter up the stairs to her room and then clatter back down again. She returns, looking much the same as when she left, just a little flushed from the exertion.

"What?" says British Queen.

May Queen stands in the centre of the room. She holds out her hand. There, in the palm, are several pieces of chalk. "I was a dressmaker's assistant," she says. "Before. In London." She walks over to the curtains and draws a huge white square with the dressmaker's chalk onto the black material. Her strokes are deft and sure. "This is the shop where I worked," she says. "In Kensington." She writes a word at the top of the square. "Durbin's. Durbin's Dress Shop." She draws a door in the shop, and then starts to draw mannequins and dresses in the shop window. "This one," she says, tapping the outline of an evening dress with her piece of chalk, "was the most gorgeous red. Velvet that was soft as fur. It was for the daughter of a magistrate. She used to arrive for her fittings in a chauffeur-driven Daimler. And this one—" She points to the chalk sketch next to the magistrate's daughter's dress. "This one was designed by Mrs. Durbin, but I chose the material for it. Jaconet. That's what I chose. Because I wanted to make a dress that felt as light as smoke, so that when you moved in it there was that lightness to you."

We watch May Queen draw the shop where she worked onto the blackout curtains. It is transfixing. How odd it is to think of our lives before we left them. Sometimes I wonder if I'll ever go back to London. If there'll be a London to go back to. And sometimes I feel the weariness of being away from home for such an indefinite stretch of time, and all I want, all I long for, is to go home. And is it a place, I think, or just a feeling? And will I ever have that feeling of home again?

"Was it bombed?" I ask. "Durbin's Dress Shop."

"Not for a long time," says May Queen. "But the shops on either side of it disappeared. Big craters in the road. One had been a stationer's, and I was always finding envelopes in the strangest places, as if someone had mysteriously left a letter between the drainpipe and the wall. Or propped up against the front window." She draws a small chalk rectangle in the bottom right corner of her shop to indicate an errant envelope. "We didn't know what to do, so we just kept coming to work. And then one day we had disappeared as well." She stands back from her sketch on the curtain. "That's what it looked like," she says. "How I remember it." She turns to face us, the chalk held between her fingers like a pen, or the stem of a rose. On her face is an expression of bewilderment, as though she can't quite believe what has happened to her life. And I realize that we haven't left our lives. They have left us. The known things in them. The structure of our days. All the bones of who we are have been removed from us. We have been abandoned by the very facts of ourselves, by the soft weight of the old world.

May Queen's real name is Alice. She stands in front of the outline of Durbin's Dress Shop, holding on to her stick of chalk. "I remember," she says, "that dress I made of jaconet. The dress that was like smoke. It was bought by a tall, thin woman. I did her fitting a few days before the shop disappeared. She was fidgety, I remember that. And she wore the dress home."

18

Mrs. Woolf is dead. It is broadcast with the war news on the evening of April 21. She has drowned in that Sussex river after all. Her body was found by children.

I cannot believe it. I don't want to believe it. I am unexpectedly angry at her for dying. And I keep confusing her death with the war dead. She died during the war, I think, pushing my head against the stiff chair back when I hear the news—not *from* the war. But what can be separated out any more? It's all the war.

I leave the wireless room, go out into the night, where the sky, weighted down with stars, sags black over the courtyard.

Dear Mrs. Woolf.

You weren't perfect. You got some things wrong in your books. I never believed the point of view from the flowers in *Kew Gardens*. Flowers would not think like that. They're not about thought at all. And I know *To the Lighthouse* was meant to be set in the Hebrides, but it couldn't have been. You got the flora wrong. There are no elms or dahlias in the Hebrides. And no carnations.

I walk over the grass of the quadrangle. It is starting to get long and should be mowed soon. I can feel it brush against the sides of my boots as I walk past the stables and through the opening out to the gardens.

Dear Mrs. Woolf.

Some of your books I didn't even like very much. I found *Night and Day* a bit dull, and *The Voyage Out* not that interesting, although I liked the part about the Thames.

I walk down to the South Garden. From there I can see the dark tilt of the fields below. I stand under a tree already delirious with blossom. The chestnut trees are out. Dear Mrs. Woolf, I think, but there is nothing really to say. The connection I felt to her words can never now be told to her. She will never know I followed her one summer evening in London through the square. She will never know how I felt when I read her books. I remember the delicious fall into *Mrs. Dalloway*, how I kept expecting the story to drop me, but it held me up, kept me buoyant.

Dear Mrs. Woolf.

There's the sound of a nightingale, rising from down near the fields. Each note as melodious as water. And then, above that sound is another sound, one I can't at first place. A thin, droning whine, growing in intensity and frequency. It's a sound I am familiar with from London. Bombers. A raid of bombers on their way to, or back from, patrolling the Devon coast. The nightingale keeps singing. I wait for it to stop, as the planes roar towards us and are then directly overhead. But the nightingale keeps up her song. Perhaps even nature has become inured to this war. Or perhaps the nightingale needs to sing so desperately that nothing will silence her. The planes pass over, high above us, and the bird keeps singing, is still singing, as I walk back up towards the buildings.

As I'm passing by the kitchen garden I see something out of the corner of my eye. A flash of white against the bricks. It's gone so fast I don't really know what to think. Only the next day, when Golden Wonder tells of having seen a figure in white moving among the trees, and the first chicken disappears, will I remember this nocturnal flicker of white and name it as a ghost.

19

There are three things left in the Garden of Longing. One is dead, and one is not yet in bloom. The last plant has grown rampant, making a great cloud of bluish pink bloom over the flower bed. Like a thousand butterflies. This is the *Rosa eglanteria*—the Sweet Briar Rose, with its small single flowers and its thick branches with hooked thorns. The thing about the Sweet Briar Rose is that while the fragrance of most roses comes from the flowers themselves, this rose stores its fragrance in its leaves. The scent is strongest after a rainfall, but if you crush a leaf between your fingers, you will release the scent of apples.

Whatever questions I answer by naming the characteristics of the plants in this garden, by attaching them to longing, other questions emerge. Did the person who planted this garden plant the Sweet Briar Rose because they wanted to remember the scent of apples, because apples figured in their story? Or was it simply a metaphor for longing—that the *Rosa eglanteria* released an unexpected fragrance, had a secret that surprised with its poignancy? I don't know what to think. And the more I find out in this garden, the less I know.

The plant not yet in bloom is lavender. I love lavender. What is more potent than to have that scent on your fingers as you leave the garden? To rub your hands over the leaves, so that all day, as you do your duties, the dying smell will remind you, will make you feel longing all over again. Dead flowers keep their fragrance. And with lavender on them, it is as though your hands become dead flowers themselves, losing the living scent little by little, spending it into the air, so it disappears and disappears.

The thing about longing is this: It is easy to feel equal to wanting. It is rare to feel equal to having.

The final plant in the Garden of Longing is dead, and has been for many years. I find evidence of it only by accident, as I'm pawing through the earth trying to free the roots of the rose from a rush of choking weeds. There, in the earth, I find a withered husk, an old corm of *Crocus sativus*—Saffron crocus.

I do not know why it is there. I cannot guess. The Saffron crocus is hard to grow, does not live very long. The spice is delicate and valuable. These things are akin to longing, I suppose, but I do not feel confident with these explanations.

On the afternoon I discover the *Crocus sativus* I stay in the garden for a long time. I have salvaged dead wood from the grove of trees behind the flower bed, have made a crude bench from this. I sit there and I look at the cascade of Sweet Briar Rose, at the brush of lavender, and I try to imagine the Saffron crocus growing between them.

I have cleared the tangle of trees above the flower bed so that now the sun moves over the garden. I can see where it falls, what it touches. There are blackbirds calling from the woods.

Later, I lie under the weight of *The Genus Rosa*, wrap my arms around the volume on my chest, and crush it against me. Ellen Willmott reminded me, when I looked through her book earlier that evening, of how the Sweet Briar was a rose used extensively by classical authors. For Shakespeare, Chaucer, and Spenser, it was the eglantine. Milton tried to use it also, but he got it confused with the woodbine. I try to remember some Milton, but can't. And then I do remember something—a line from Virgil's *Georgics*, and I know that I've found my answer to the Saffron crocus. It might not be the right answer, what was originally intended, but it satisfies me, and this, I realize, under the heavy assurance of *The Genus Rosa*, is what should matter.

"Let there be gardens to tempt them, breathing saffron flowers."

20

I ask the Lumper the question I need to ask her, and then I go and find Jane in the stables. She is grooming the young horse and seems so absorbed in her task that I don't want to break this moment with my demands.

"Jane," I finally say, and she looks up.

"Hello, Gwen," she says, and smiles.

"In the absence of a motor car, I need a horse and cart," I say. "Would you drive me to town?"

"What for?"

"I'll tell you on the way." I put my hand into my trouser pocket where I have stashed the pay for being a Land Girl that Mrs. Billings gave me last week. I hope it is enough to buy what I need.

"Tell me now," says Jane. She puts down the brush. "Why do I have to wait?"

I don't want to tell her yet. "Just drive me," I say, rather irritably.

"Chickens," says Jane. "You must be after some more chickens."

Two chickens have disappeared from the coop now, and the others seem very distressed and aren't laying as much as usual. "No, it's not chickens. Nothing to do with chickens, in fact. I'll tell you when we get there," I say, because by then I'll have to. It will be obvious.

"Oh, all right." Jane opens the door of the stall and steps out towards me. She seems so small and known. I know her, I think, as she walks out from behind the wooden stall door. Just a little, but I do know something about her. We know something of each other. And the thing is that I like her; what I know of her I like. Before arriving at Mosel, I'm not sure I ever liked anyone. Roy Peake very briefly, but that seems so long ago now, and he quickly became hugely disappointing.

"What's the matter with you?" says Jane. "You've gone all moody looking. Do you want to go to town or stand there and cry?"

"Go to town," I say. And we do.

I feel nervous on our return, as we drive up the hill to the big house. What if my bright idea wasn't such a good one after all? But it's too late for nervous speculation. We are driving up the hill with the cart creaking under the weight of its newly purchased cargo.

No one answers my cautious knock at the front door, so Jane and I go on into the house. There's a soldier writing letters in the dining room. "Captain Raley?" I ask, and he points upstairs.

"Listen," says Jane, when we're back in the hall and I'm making a beeline for the staircase. "I'll meet you outside. I want to have a look round for David."

"Are you sure that's a good idea?" I remember how

upset she was the night we came up to the house for the dance.

Jane tries to smile at me but can't quite manage it. "It's not an idea," she says. "That's the trouble." She touches me lightly on the arm, as though I'm the one who needs the reassurance. "I'll see you outside."

Raley is in the upstairs study. He's sitting by the fire, reading a book.

"I thought you gave up on poetry," I say.

"I did." Raley flashes the book cover at me. *Concise British Flora*. "I thought that, since I'm here, I should learn something about the place."

"Come outside. I've got something for you."

"Ah, Gwen. Bossy as usual." Raley lays his book aside and follows me downstairs and out to the horse and cart, waiting on the driveway. Sitting on the bare boards of the cart, its roots wrapped in burlap, is the magnolia tree I have bought from the nursery just outside of town.

"It will keep pace with your loss," I say. "You need something to cast a shadow and lose its fragrance to the earth."

Raley says nothing, just stands beside me, looking at the tree in the cart.

"I'm sorry," I say. "It's already bloomed for this year." It would have flared up a month ago, dropped its waxy cache of petals to the ground in glorious failure.

Raley is still silent. I had thought about this so carefully, and yet I must have been wrong. It has been the wrong thing to do. I think of that night in the house when he and I stood in the doorway of the kitchen, watching Jane cut David's hair. How I had felt the solid wall of him behind me and how all I wanted to do was to lean back against him. "I'm sorry," I say again, for I feel now I should apologize for ever having thought this up.

"Gwen." He puts his hand on my arm, and when I turn to face him I see that he is near to crying. "Don't apologize. Please don't do that. I love magnolias. And they won't have come into bloom yet in Toronto, where I'm from." He squeezes my arm gently. "I like how sad they are," he says. "Sad candles, that's what they look like. A magnolia is a tree lit with sad candles."

Raley wants to plant the magnolia so that he can see it from his room at Mosel. We dig the hole at the front of the house, right under his window. Raley does most of the work of digging, leaning hard into the shovel with the full weight of his body. I have never seen such a beautiful man. His muscles move like water under his skin.

"That's deep enough," I say finally, even though I would like to continue the pleasure of watching him work.

Raley rests on his shovel. There's sweat on his face. He has his shirt sleeves rolled up and the veins on his forearms and the backs of his hands stand out from the effort of digging. He wipes his forehead on his arm.

"I was meant to work in a bank," he says. "Doesn't that seem strange now?" He doesn't wait or even look at me for an answer. "But my friends were going to war and convinced me that because of my university education I'd get a better deal as an officer." Raley turns and looks at me now. "There was a magnolia tree outside that bank I was meant to work at. A magnificent tree. I would have passed by it twice a day." Raley brushes his hands together to clean them of earth. "Perhaps I could have been happy doing that. Do you think so, Gwen?" He seems like an anxious little boy when he asks this. I want to jump down into the hole and put my arms around him, but instead, alarmed at the thought, I back up and hit my head on the magnolia tree.

"I don't think a tree can give meaning to your life," I say, rubbing the back of my head.

But I am wrong about this. I will be proven wrong by this very magnolia tree that we are planting.

"What happened to your friend?" I ask.

Raley looks at the earth at his feet, jabs at it with the blade of the shovel. "Shot by accident," he says. "Before he even got to the war. We joined up together and he was killed in a training accident."

"And you were sent here." I look up at the house, how grand it is, how it belongs to another way of life entirely. "How long ago?"

"A week before that day I saw you at the station," he says. "What does that make it? A month? Yesterday? A hundred years ago?" Raley stabs his shovel into the pile of earth at the edge of the hole, and then he slowly raises his arms into branches above his head.

We look at each other, and I retrieve the shovel from the side of the hole, gently push a bit of earth down into the cavity. Enough to cover his shoes.

After the magnolia has been planted, Raley and I sit in the sun on the front step of the house, watching the new tree. It feels as though we are waiting for it to grow before our eyes, sprout up like a tree in a fairy tale. Up and up, into the clouds, piercing the underside of heaven itself.

"There were magnolias in the London squares I used to walk through," I say, thinking of how there was a magnolia in almost every one of the squares in Bloomsbury, threading them together in my mind. Each green page illuminated by the light of a magnolia tree. Where were they now? Blown to pieces, I expect.

"Do you miss London?" asks Raley.

"More than anything."

"Tell me something."

I close my eyes and think of the river. I think of walking across Waterloo Bridge and seeing the distant lamps of Westminster, the close lights of Hungerford Bridge. The river is grey at night, a shiver of grey under the bridge. "Sometimes," I say, "I used to go down to the Thames at low tide and collect the bits of old clay pipes that would wash up against the pilings. There were so many of these tiny hollow tubes. They were like bird bones. I liked to think of all those people, those men of a hundred years ago, dropping those pipes into the river. I liked that in the modern city, with all its bustle and clatter, I could be engaged in a private work of archaeological excavation." I open my eyes and look at the magnolia tree. It does seem to have grown. I have left all those bits of pilfered pipe in my office at the Royal Horticultural Society. Until this moment I had forgotten that, but now I can clearly see them on the little shelf just inside the door, neatly arranged according to size, looking like a miniature clay xylophone. "I'm afraid that when I go back, when the war ends—if the war ends—everything I've loved will have disappeared."

"I have the opposite problem," says Raley, looping his arms around his knees. "I'm fairly certain Toronto will have remained intact. It's more likely that I will disappear."

I look at Captain Raley, sitting next to me on the step in the April sun. He has the kind of blond hair that will bleach white in summer. I look at the fine hairs on the back of his wrist, his neatly cut nails now all grubby with dirt from planting the tree. His hands look like my hands now. I like that. "Tell me something," I say.

"The best view of Toronto," says Raley, "is from the islands that lie the other side of the harbour. There's a ferry that runs between the islands and the mainland. That was where I first met Peter, my friend who died. We were eight years old. We had both wandered away from our respective parents and met on the upper deck, near the front of the ferry. We stood against the railing. I will always remember this. The top of the railing was smooth, dark wood, and big around as my leg. There were gulls above the waves. We stood side by side, no small talk, and then Peter said, quite solemnly, 'Let's take our coats off and throw them in the sea.' And of course it wasn't really the sea, but the lake is so big that it feels like the sea. And so we did this. By the time my mother caught up to us, we were struggling out of our shirts." Raley turns to me then and smiles. I can see his perfect teeth. The lines around his eyes crinkle up with his smile. He has no wrinkles on his forehead. All the lines on his face are from smiling, from laughter, from being happy.

21

I lie under *The Genus Rosa* and imagine it's Captain Raley on top of me, squashing the life out of me. I have a bath before dinner, look at my body critically through the bathwater. It's milky white as a slug. No one's ever really seen it. I might as well have lived underground all this time, wriggling around, sucking mouthfuls of dirt. I dry myself roughly with the stiff, nubby towel, and suddenly my feet seem horrifically ugly. Why have I never noticed this before?

At dinner, my knee presses against the table and I feel an incredible wave of desire. When I pull my chair in closer to the table, the edge of the tabletop pushes against my stomach and I almost can't breathe.

"What is the matter with you?" whispers Jane from beside me.

"Nothing."

"Are you drunk?"

"Of course not." I look at her in alarm. Surely I'm not as bad as all that. "Step on my foot," I say.

"Why?"

"Just do it."

Jane regards me with bemused confusion, but she does as I ask, stamps down hard on my foot that's closest to hers. I cry out, and the other girls stop talking.

"Thank you," I say to Jane. "It's fine now." And it is. I have replaced one kind of pain with another and my equilibrium has returned. I eat my dinner with renewed appetite, and then, since Jane's not hungry, I eat most of hers as well.

After dinner we go and listen to the war broadcast. London is burning again. Masses of incendiary bombs fell during the night and the fires raged against all effort to control them. Westminster Hall was hit, and the Abbey, and the Houses of Parliament themselves. I am very grateful not to have been there to witness the destruction of these familiar landmarks. At least I can remember them as they were.

The other item of news tonight is not nearly so distressing. It seems that on the night of the worst bombing of London so far, Rudolph Hess, the deputy fuehrer of Germany, flew a fighter plane to Scotland on a mission to broker peace between his nation and ours. He was guided on the nine-hundred-mile journey by two compasses strapped to the legs of his trousers, and by the dance music from a Danish radio station. He was looking for the home of the Duke of Hamilton, whom he'd met once years before, and who he was convinced would understand his mission of peace. Unable to land the plane, he flew it upside down so he would drop out of the cockpit, opened his parachute and landed in a field, where he was apprehended by a farmer in his underwear who had been awakened by the noise of the crashing plane.

"Good to know this war is driving them insane as well," says Jane.

I look around the room at the girls. Here we are, crowded round the wireless, like any family anywhere in Britain. Behind us the blackout curtains are dripping with our stories. British Queen has drawn a picture of her family home in London, complete with drawings of the members of her family in the various rooms. "I miss them," she said when she drew this, and I realized how young these girls are and how, for most of them, it's their first time away from their homes and families.

Golden Wonder has drawn her favourite meal, composed of food that has become almost impossible to procure since the start of war. It could be years before she can glut herself on cheese again. Or tins of condensed milk. Or puddings made with heaps of sugar. She draws the plate of food and then, above it, she draws the individual items on the plate and labels them accordingly. It looks a lot like a diagram in a nutrition pamphlet.

Salad Blue has drawn the London Zoo. It is the place she loves most in the world, she said. No one asked how many places in the world she had been to. Her lion and tiger peer balefully out from behind their cage bars. The largest section of her drawing is given over to a wolf, drawn in profile, pacing in his prison. "I liked the wolf best of all," she said. "At night, sometimes, when the moon was full, he would howl. In the middle of London there could be a howling wolf. Think of that." Salad Blue had carefully traced the shape of the wolf as though she wanted to get every contour of his form right. The white-chalk wolf looked almost ready to howl, pacing up and down the permanent night of the blackout curtain at Mosel. In the bottom corner of the wolf's cage, Salad Blue had drawn the sign that was affixed to the cage of the wolf at the Regent Park Zoo. "Do not touch this animal," the sign says. "But I did," said Salad Blue proudly when she added the sign to her drawing. "He rubbed his sides against the cage bars and I scratched him behind the ears, like a dog."

I remember the first day I was at Mosel, how I wandered through the girls' bedrooms, looking for one that was free. The room with the stuffed dog must have been Salad Blue's.

Victualette Noir draws the kitchen of her father's hotel in London. She draws herself in at all the workstations. "That's me," she says. "Making pâté. And there I am puréeing vegetables." She is the worst illustrator of the lot of us. Her self-portraits look like an electrified cat, a kitchen utensil, and a letter from the Chinese alphabet.

There are only three stories left to be told—the Lumper, Jane, and myself. Tonight, after the wireless has been turned off, May Queen holds the dressmaker's chalk out to Jane. "Your turn," she suggests, but Jane shakes her head no.

"Why not?" asks Salad Blue.

Jane looks at the section of curtain that's been designated as hers. "I like it black," she says. "I like it as it is."

"I'll go." The Lumper swipes the chalk out of May Queen's hand. She is bursting with her good idea. The first few times we engaged in this storytelling, she looked positively stricken that she might be called upon to tell something of herself, and that she had no notion of what to say. But now she knows. She draws five long, sideways parallel lines. One of them, propelled by the Lumper's enthusiastic rendering, goes right through the wall of Victualette's hotel and spears the brain of the electrified cat making pâté.

"Careful," warns Victualette. "That's my head."

But the Lumper is oblivious to her clumsiness. Her arm is positively lyrical as she sweeps it along in pursuit of her line.

"This is the piece of music I've been learning to play," she says, and starts dabbing great circular notes onto the bars. "I'm not very good at it, but I do know it by heart." She draws a tail on each note, an upward flourish, like a wing.

It is strange to think of the Lumper playing the piano, sitting poised on a bench, stretching her huge hands over the span of keys.

"What's the piece?" asks Golden Wonder, and Doris writes the name of the composer, Ravel, and the word "Pavane" under the bar of musical score. "It's got a long, funny name I can't say," she tells us. "But it means 'Dance for the Dead Princess.'" She stands proudly beside the bit of music she's written out. The bit of music she's given us, suspended in this room, in the air we breathe, for as long as we are here.

"Doesn't it sound lovely?" she says.

22

Another chicken disappears.

"This has got to stop," I say at breakfast, after Victualette Noir has reported this fact.

"Well, don't look at me," says Salad Blue. "I don't even like chicken. Or eggs, either, if you want to know." She goes back to scraping her toast with margarine.

Now that the chickens are once again trouble, no one has time for their predicament. There was one brief day, when Victualette Noir made an omelette for supper, that I was popular.

After breakfast I go out to the chicken coop to see if I can find any evidence of the missing chicken. But, as with the other two chickens, this one has just vanished, leaving no clues behind. There are no feathers or blood to suggest a fox. I poke my head into the coop itself and the hens squawk and flap at me. Have they seen a ghost? How could I possibly tell this? "Animal, vegetable, or mineral?" I say to the nearest chicken, and she pecks me on the hand. I back out and hit my head on the top of the entrance.

"Any luck?" I jump at the voice behind me. It's Jane. She's standing on the path, smoking a cigarette.

"No."

"Ghost," she says calmly.

"That's so ridiculous," I say, rubbing the back of my head with my hand. I'm bound to get a lump. "How can it possibly be a ghost?"

"Don't you believe in anything you can't see, Gwen?"

"No." I'm starting to feel irritable because of banging my head. "Well, yes." Seeds, I think. Love. "But not ghosts," I say.

Jane throws her cigarette end on the path. "Ghosts are the easy part," she says. "How to keep someone alive is more difficult."

"Is that what you are doing?" I ask. "Keeping Andrew alive?"

"Yes."

I let myself out of the hen run and walk over to join Jane on the path. She looks particularly tired this morning. The natural light of England is blue. There is a slight blue mist over everything all of the time. When the sky is dark, as it is today, this is very evident. Blue light makes Jane look worn out.

"How do you do it, then?" I ask. "Keep him alive?" I am actually thinking more of the chickens at this moment—of how to keep them alive, keep them from disappearing.

"Write letters to him in my head. Think of him always and everywhere. Love him fiercely and absolutely. Believe him alive." Jane looks at me, the blue light sad on her skin. "What else can I do?" she says.

I can see the tension in her, how her small body is a thin, tight wire she is keeping ready for Andrew to make his way across. Back to her. There is nothing I can say to calm her, so instead I turn her gently with my hand on her back and we walk together out of the garden.

We meet May Queen in the quadrangle, on her way to work in the North Garden. "Did you find the ghost?" she asks.

"There is no ghost." How many more times must I repeat this? I feel like stamping my foot.

"Ghost," Jane whispers to May Queen.

I walk with Jane to the stables, then leave her there and head back to the west wing. With all my interest in the lost garden, I have been neglecting my domestic chores. My room is cluttered. My clothes are in need of laundering.

As I'm passing by the arch I hear a noise from the driveway. Marching feet. I look through and see the column of Canadian soldiers, each one wearing a rucksack. They are headed down the hill. Raley is at the front of the column. He is training them after all. I want to wave to him, but he doesn't see me standing on the cobblestones under the arch. Eyes front, he and the other men march past me, on down the hill.

I spend the morning washing my clothes. Then, after they are hung to dry and all the mess in my room has been herded into new order, I go to the kitchen, scavenge an apple and a couple of biscuits, and make for the garden.

It is a grey, windy day. The sky seems low enough to touch. It has rained while I've been indoors. I walk through the orchard. There are blossoms on the fruit trees. They scatter their scent upon me as I walk beneath them. I think of the Garden of Longing, of the Sweet Briar Rose and how it smells of apples when wet.

Was the person who made that garden saying something about the orchard? Was the planting of the garden a kind of map? But the more I explore of the garden and its associations, the more the line is blurred between what is the gardener's story and what is mine. Planting a garden is about making a series of choices, and then the interpretation of those choices also becomes a series of choices. I need to know more about the person who made the garden or I won't be able to decipher any more from the choices that were made there.

I walk past the espaliered apple trees along the orchard wall. They reach out their twisted limbs to me. But they have been too long trained to the wall. They need that structure and support. Even if they were cut loose from the wires, they would still choose to grow up against the stone.

I turn the corner of the wall, to enter the yew walk and leave the orchard behind, when I suddenly see it huge above me. An angel. A green angel. One of the giant yews has been clipped into the shape of an angel. The body is slight, flares out at the base. The wings are huge, muscled out from the shoulders, two majestic sweeps of green. The head is round and without features, merely there for balance of the whole. It is the wings that are the overwhelming aspect of this living sculpture.

I stand in front of it. On the other side of this topiary angel is my hidden garden. But no, I slip through the hedge and look at the angel from behind. It is on the edge of the woods, one of the first yews on the path. The garden would remain out of sight to anyone clipping the yew.

Back up at the stables Jane is putting fresh straw down for the horses. She has her back to me.

"What's the angel for?" I ask.

"How do you know it was me?" she says, not turning around from her task.

How do I know it was her? "It didn't occur to me it could be anyone else," I say. "No one else knows me as well." I want to say, *cares about me*, but what if this isn't true and Jane only humours me because she's bored with the others?

Jane stabs her pitchfork into the pile of straw. The stables seem very quiet and still with the animals out grazing the South Garden. "Come on," she says.

We stand on the yew walk, under the green angel. The sun has appeared for a moment and rests on one of the wings.

"I've only ever cut hair before," says Jane, squinting up at the angel. "But it's not bad, is it?"

"What's it for?" I still don't understand why Jane would take a perfectly good morning and use it to fashion this piece of hedge into a heavenly creature.

"It's for you," she says simply. "To keep you company. I know you're always down here by the orchard, on your solitary secret missions." Jane reaches a hand up to her creation and touches the tip of a wing. "A sentry," she says. "Someone to watch over you, so you don't get lonely."

I look up at the angel. I don't know what to say. I hope that Jane hasn't seen the garden that lies behind the hedge. But maybe, even if she had, she wouldn't think much of it. It is an odd collection of plants, and the words that define the garden, that give it context, are not that visible, being jammed into the soil at the edge of the bed.

"Why an angel?" I ask.

"Well, I can't very well do a ghost," she says. "It wouldn't be very visually impressive." She looks over at me. "Don't you like it?"

It's not that I don't like it. There's something lovely about this massive hedge suddenly becoming something other. It's like a silent crowd of people and one of them spontaneously breaking into song. So, it's not that. It's more that I don't know what to make of Jane for doing this.

"Well," says Jane. "It was a challenge to see if I could hone something from all this green. That's all." She looks away from me. I have taken too long to reply to her question.

"I like it very much," I say, but it is too late for that now. It sounds completely insincere.

"The thing about angels," says Jane, "is that they can read one another's thoughts."

I try not to think of anything. The sun flickers out behind a cloud. The patch of light lifts from the angel's wing.

"Andrew and I used to discuss angels," says Jane. "When we were reading philosophy at university."

This surprises me. I had assumed that Jane, like the other girls, was from working-class roots.

"I didn't know you went to university. I thought you were a hairdresser in London."

"That was after."

"After what?"

Jane fishes a cigarette out from under her jumper. She

has spent her entire pay from the Land Army on Gold Flakes. When we went to town for the magnolia tree, she cashed her pay and exchanged it all for packets of cigarettes. "I got a bit overwhelmed in university," she says. "I had to stop going."

"What do you mean by 'overwhelmed'?"

Jane lights her cigarette. "My nerves were under great strain. That's how it was phrased at the time." She looks at me, expelling a stream of smoke. "Breakdown, Gwen," she says. "I had a breakdown."

The angel regards us sternly from the top of the hedge.

"Why?" I ask. "What happened?"

"I realized I wasn't the brightest person there, and I just couldn't go on, knowing that. Somehow it made everything seem so futile." Jane looks at me. "Sounds rather pathetic, doesn't it? But I need to be right next to something, right up against it. No gaps. And if I couldn't be the one right next to knowledge, then I didn't exist at all. That's how it is with me."

This is a hard way to live, to feel. I can't imagine living at the end of my nerves like that. At the end of my limits. I have never had to be the best at anything. I could *never* be the best at anything. I am certainly not the best gardener, and never have been, although I do have an instinctive affinity for plants. I do know this.

"Tell me something else about angels," I say.

Jane brushes a piece of hair out of her eyes, gazes up at her topiary creation. "You'll like this," she says. "One of the debates by the thirteenth-century theologians was whether angels belonged to the same species, or whether each individual angel was a species of its own." She looks over at me. "A great mystery. The genus angel."

23

My mother was very beautiful. Even when she was dying. She had wanted to go on the stage and couldn't, because of me, but that desire had remained, become part of her character. Wherever she was, it was as if she was just about to be called onstage to deliver her lines. There was always an air of anticipation about her. The expectation of applause.

There are many ways to tell a story. In opposition to. In sympathy with. What to leave out. What to put in.

My mother was beautiful. I was always plain. "How could I have produced such a creature?" she said more than once. Some days she locked me outside because she couldn't bear to look at me. I played in the gardens, among the flowers of white and blue—the same colours my mother used to like to wear. I would chase after her in the house sometimes, anxious when she left a room without me. Her flowing dresses of white and blue waving up ahead of me like semaphore.

My mother was beautiful. I can never get away from that fact. If there is one thing to say about my mother, that is it. And whatever choices I make in telling my mother's story, this is the soil they are planted in. My mother was beautiful.

No one knows why she married my father, a much older friend of her father's. Money? Safety? The idea that the security offered within such a marriage would allow her the chance to pursue her artistic ambitions? He had once told her she had "dramatic arms." What she said about the marriage to me was, "It was a moment of weakness." And I always knew I was the product of that weakness. My mother became pregnant. My father died. All her hopes of becoming an actress were emptied.

The moment opens. The moment closes. There is sunlight. There is frost. There is the brief idea of roses amid the patch of weeds.

I thought that if I could cure my diseased parsnips in the Royal Horticultural Society laboratory, I could cure my mother's cancer in hospital. I know there was no real link between those two things, but I felt that there was. Instinct and wish. How to pull them apart.

I often didn't go to visit my mother in hospital in favour of staying in the lab at night, staring at my jars of parsnips, making my detailed notes that became, in the end, just a catalogue of death. All I was doing, really, was watching something die.

"You're not taking care of me," my mother would whisper, when I did go and see her. But this refrain on the edge of death had also been her refrain from life. She would say it to butchers and taxi drivers, to shop assistants and waiters. And always to me. I did my best. I did. But what could I give my mother that would make up for the fact that my birth, my existence, had denied her the life she could have given herself?

My mother locked me outdoors and her love denied became my profession. The garden became my home. I would lie on my back in the grass near the beds, name the flowers that swayed tall above me in the sun. Phlox. Foxglove. Hollyhock. Each name a word that opened the moment. I lay on my back at the edge of the flowers. I knew what to do to take care of them. It was easy to learn this. The simple tasks required to keep the garden alive and thriving were easy to master, and always effective.

There are many different stories to tell. It's never the same. Every day weather blows in and out, alters the surface. Sometimes it is stripped down to a single essential truth, the thing that is always believed, no matter what. The seeds from which the garden has grown.

My mother was beautiful.

I ruined her life.

24

The Garden of Loss blooms in May. It is a simpler construction than the Garden of Longing. It contains fewer species, but more plants. The middle of the three gardens, it begins with a great, breaking wave of peonies. The blooms are white and pale pink, grow upright for now, giant buttons of brilliance festooning green leafy tunics. But soon their heads will become too heavy for the thin, weed-like stalks on which they rise with such hope, and the peonies will crash to the ground in a wave of grief. They are too much for themselves, and soon they know it. I have always loved peonies. There is something almost heroic in their reckless collapse. And there is nothing sadder than a crowd of stricken peonies, their heads full of rain.

The more time I spend studying and tending this garden, the more respect I have for whoever planted it. What they knew of longing was that it sprang from the earth at odd moments, unplanned and unexpected, borne on different carriers. But loss was more uniform than that. It surged up and carried one along. Loss was a choir. Loss moved in harmony. It struggled heavenward. It crashed to earth.

The tag for "Loss" is scratched onto a metal stake, jammed into the earth in front of the low wall of peonies. The word is written vertically.

Behind the peonies are clumps of purple irises. There are many varieties of iris and I am required to take a specimen back to my room in order to identify it from my reference books. *Iris graminea.* This iris likes to grow in leafy soil in partial shade, making it well suited to this flower bed hewn out of the surrounding woodland. What distinguishes this iris from others is that the flowers smell like plums. After reading this in my book I think of the Sweet Briar Rose with its apple-scented foliage. Surely this cannot be mere coincidence? Having seen how carefully this garden has been planted, I have to believe there must be a connection between those two plants, and a reference to something else, something unknown to me. Something outside the confines of the garden.

I walk through the orchard. The apple trees are just stepping out of their blossom. There are a few plum trees near the stone wall. I stand under them. I move around them, searching their bark and limbs for evidence. But there is nothing for me to find. Or perhaps, because I don't know what I'm looking for, I have missed it altogether. I look up through the twisted branches to the patch of blue sky overhead. Did lovers meet here? Was that it? Why couldn't I look up into the crown of this tree and see all the words ever said beneath it etched into the purple bark? Nature is a mute witness and therefore, for me now, completely unreliable.

What I can't decide from studying the garden is whether it was planted to remember somebody or something, or to show somebody. Was it for someone? And who was it for?

There is one final planting in the Garden of Loss. It is not nearly as dramatic as the other two groupings of flowers. A straggly clutch of potentillas, growing next to the majestic rush of irises. But these potentillas draw me closer than ever to the invisible gardener, make our connection more certain and alarming. The flowers have the proper name of *Potentilla nepalensis*. They are commonly called "Miss Willmott," after Ellen Willmott, author of *The Genus Rosa*.

25

Ellen Willmott had been a gardener since she was a child. As a daughter of wealthy parents, she had the money to indulge her passion, to finance all her fertile schemes. She also inherited the large family home, Warley Place, where she put many of her gardening dreams into action. Unmarried, wealthy, and with a passion to drive her, she had a free and purposeful life. An enviable life.

Miss Willmott had a long history with the Royal Horticultural Society, and it was from this part of her life that I had my connection with her. She had been a long-standing member of the Narcissus and Tulip Committee and her earliest fame was as a daffodil grower and hybridizer. At gardening college, and later, when I worked at the Royal Horticultural Society, I frequently heard her referred to as the greatest woman gardener who ever lived. The 'Queen of Spades.'

The potentilla in the Garden of Loss is not the only plant to be named after this famous and enthusiastic gardener. There are dahlias, narcissus, a peony, lily, delphinium, iris. And there are the roses that bear her name, for roses were her true passion. Roses were the flower, out of all the others she tended and cultivated, that she truly loved.

The Genus Rosa was Ellen Willmott's testimony to her passion for roses. A tremendously ambitious undertaking, it was to be a comprehensive listing of all the roses in existence, including the genetics of every rose, its derivation and its kin. All known botanical and historical detail was to have been included in this magnum opus. She intended it to be the definitive work on the genus rosa.

The enterprise was a struggle from the start. Miss Willmott began the work in 1901, at the age of forty-three. She had trouble collaborating with her illustrator, who she felt was not painting the ideal example of each rose. She had difficulty enticing a publisher to invest in so huge and costly a venture. She ended up by partially subsidizing the production of the book herself. In 1910 the first volume was released, and in 1914, the second. Initial sales were disappointing, and then the advent of the war scuttled the whole project. Ellen Willmott, never one to economize, was bankrupted by the war and by her failure to curb her extravagance. Although she managed to hang on to her house, she sold a lot of her possessions and couldn't even afford to keep a gardener on, so that the once beautiful grounds of Warley disintegrated into a ruined paradise.

Sometimes our passion is our ruin.

The thing with roses is that they were just too unmanageable for Ellen Willmott—indeed, for any single person—to pin down and categorize, to fix on the page. They kept fluctuating, changing their names and associations, refusing to lie still. The roses kept growing, even on paper. They were a living language. And Ellen Willmott couldn't hope to contain them.

The Genus Rosa is peppered with names of roses with a line drawn through them and then another name written in over the original. All of Miss Willmott's life had been in service to roses, and to find that this seemingly simple task of classification was impossible must have been devastating. Surely understanding provides mastery. Isn't that what we want to believe? Isn't that how we explain our very lives?

What I love about *The Genus Rosa* is that it got away. That even with a lover as devout and determined as Miss Willmott, it would not be tamed into human hands, into this human world.

Near the end of her life—she must have been in her mid-seventies at the time—Ellen Willmott gave a lecture at the Royal Horticultural Society that I attended. She was on the Lily Committee at this point, and so the talk was on lilies. This is where I was going, that night I walked through London, that night I followed the ghostly figure of Virginia Woolf through Tavistock Square.

The thing about Ellen Willmott that is not well known—or if it is, is never given much consequence—is that her deepest and most important relationship in life was with her younger sister. That sister's name was Rose.

The language of roses shifts like sand under our feet. It blows in and out like the wind. It carries the fragrance of the flower and then it is gone. *Rugosa. Canina. Arvensis.* It is how we learn to speak about something that is disappearing as we say its name. It is a trick, a false comfort. *Humilis.* It is what we think we need to know and how we think it needs to be known. *Involuta.* It is where we want to go, this name, and stay there, safely held forever. *Inodora. Alba. Sancta.*

26

The girls are running out of things to do. The agricultural labour that in the beginning seemed so daunting, and which they once so fiercely resisted, has been dispatched with alarming efficiency and expediency. The North Garden has been cultivated and planted with potatoes. The kitchen garden is fully under control. When I make one of my rare visits to that walled space I find the girls stretched out on blankets in their underclothes, sunbathing. My lieutenant, the Lumper, is fast asleep on a bench by the runner beans. The girls eye me with a weary reluctance as I step over their beached bodies on my way to Doris.

The Lumper is too big for the bench. Her calves and feet hinge over the end of the stone, so that her body has followed the contours of the bench and she has become a fleshy sort of bench herself. I shake her by the shoulder and she bolts awake.

"Oh," she says, straining upright. "I must have dozed off. It's very hot today. I'm sure I was only out for a moment. Before that I was pruning." There are no secateurs anywhere in sight.

"It's all right," I say. "I know there's not much to do now. I must look into that. But first—" I sit down on the bench beside her. "First I have to ask you a favour."

"What?" She looks at me with relief. Doris is always so worried about getting in trouble. I thought it would have helped, her being in charge of the others, but she hasn't taken to authority very well. She seems mostly fretful, except for the night she wrote out her piece of music on the blackout curtain. Then she seemed happy. "There is a piano at the house," I say. "You might be able to practise up there. I haven't seen anyone else using that piano." Mostly I've been there to see Raley and haven't concerned myself with anything else.

"You want me to play the 'Princess' piece for you?" Doris looks at me suspiciously.

"No, no. Never mind." Now I'm thinking of Raley, have to drag my mind back to the reason I had for seeking Doris out today. "It's not about music," I say. "I want you to ask your father to come and see me. Will you do that? I have some questions about the estate that he might know the answers to."

"Oh, yes," says Doris. "He's been asking me that himself. I think he's dying for a look round."

"Good. I'll leave it to you, then." The Lumper may not be very good at dispensing authority, but she is good at following orders. I look over at the other girls, napping in the sun. "One thing you could do," I say, "that probably wouldn't meet with much resistance, is to decorate the dining hall for the dance tonight. That would stir their torpid flesh." It is the soldiers' turn to visit our humble abode, and I know it is one thing in the immediate future that the girls are looking forward to.

"All right," says Doris, doubtfully.

"They'll want to," I say as I get up from the bench. "It

won't be a bit like asking them to prune. You'll see." I leave her to struggle with her anxiety about how to give an order, and go back to the Garden of Loss.

I am hoping that Doris's father will have a clear and vivid recollection of what the estate was like before the Great War. That he will remember the men who were employed here, details of their characters and lives. And that he will be able to tell me enough so that I can work out who made this lost garden. And why. It is impossible now to be satisfied with the anonymity of the creator. I won't rest until I've learnt all there is to know. Perhaps, I think, with surprise, I am falling in love with the garden.

The Lumper needn't have worried. The girls are only too happy to decorate for the dance with the Canadian soldiers. They have chalked stars and a moon on the blackout curtains. Tables and chairs have been moved aside to create a generous area for dancing. When I come into the dining hall the hour before the men are due to arrive, it looks wonderful. Someone has woven a nice criss-cross of branches over the fireplace mantel. The floor has been swept.

All the girls are off having their baths, or dressing for the evening. I place the flowers I have brought in their pail inside the fireplace hearth. I have cut some of the pink and white peonies from the Garden of Loss. They look soft, almost buttery, in the low light of the room.

Will Raley come? I would be a fool to think he would ever dance with me, but will he come and stand by the soft light of these flowers in this room of white stars?

Most of the other girls have clothes of their own with them, clothes appropriate for an evening such as this.

May Queen even has a beautiful blue dress from the dress shop where she once worked. Only Doris and I wear our regulation Land Army trousers and shirts. Even Jane wears several of her own jumpers over her dungarees. "I'm always cold," she says in response to my saying that she must be boiling under all those layers.

The truth is that the Land Army uniform is smarter looking than any of my ordinary clothes. I don't know what the Lumper's excuse is, though I suspect she just really likes the uniform and wants to be in it all the time. She probably sleeps with her green armlet on.

We hear the music before we see the men. They have brought the windup Victrola with them and are playing it as they walk down the road from the house. We stand very still in the hall and hear the approach of the soldiers as a thin thread of music, unwinding in the dark. It is almost like birdsong and, like birdsong, we listen to it attentively because we don't know when it might stop.

Raley does come. He leads the parade of men and gramophone up the stone steps and into the dining hall. He looks lovely. I know this is not the sort of thing one thinks about a man, let alone says to him, but he does. He looks lovely.

There are some soldiers I don't recognize from the last dance. New additions to the community at the big house. They stay back at first, shyly, but that only lasts as long as it takes for the dancing to begin. The soldiers outnumber the girls by at least three to one, so while the girls are always dancing, there is always a clutch of men standing around smoking cigarettes.

Jane doesn't dance. She and David are sitting at a

table, as far away from everyone else as they can possibly get.

"It looks beautiful," says Raley. He is suddenly beside me. I can feel the heat of his body next to mine. "I like the flowers," he says. "They look like promises, don't they? Like soft promises here in this darkened room."

"Are you sure you've gone off poetry?" I say.

He laughs and passes his flask over to me. "Go on, Gwen," he says. "Be a devil."

I swallow a hot balloon of alcohol. Whisky? Brandy? I'm so unaccustomed to drinking that I'm not exactly sure what it is. But whatever it is, I feel a flush right away. I remember my evening with the Tulip and Narcissus Committee and feel I must warn Raley of the possible consequences of giving me alcohol. "I'm liable to get very sincere," I say, "and there's a good chance I will mention parsnips. More than once."

Raley laughs again. "You're in fine form tonight," he says. "I didn't want to come to this dance, but you've redeemed the evening for me." He passes the flask my way again and I swallow gratefully.

There's a burst of clapping and we both watch as May Queen dances the length of a table and back again. Once more to applause and then she launches herself from the table into the arms of a tall man with dark hair. He catches her deftly, swings her around, and sets her safely on the ground.

"Dancing fools," says Raley. It is almost a sneer.

"You don't dance?" I am disappointed. Even though I'd tried not to wish for it, I had hoped that Raley would ask me to dance, especially since he seemed to be enjoying my company so much.

Raley holds out the flask to me again. I shouldn't, but do. I take it and drink, pass it back. "I choose my moments to be falling-down drunk," he says. "I'm allowed two a month. Dancing would increase the number, make it noticeable."

"Make what noticeable?"

"For your ears only, Gwen," says Raley. "Most of the time I am just drunk enough to balance on the line."

"What line?" I like how he says my name, softly but with a little snap at the end. Like wind in the trees, I think, and then can't recall what we're talking about. "What wind?" I say, but he's already in the middle of answering my first question and doesn't hear me.

"The line between remembering and forgetting," he says.

I can't drink any more. I feel as if I'm a tree being blown by the wind. "Am I swaying?" I ask Raley.

"Oh, Gwen," he says, and I just want him to keep on saying my name in that nice Canadian way. But he takes me by the elbow and leads me out of the dancing fray, over to a table. "Come and sit down."

It's the same table that Jane and David are at. They're at one end, huddled close together, side by side. We sit at the other end, opposite one another. Jane is blocking David from my view, but I can see the flicker of something, can see his arms moving up and down. "What's he doing?" I say.

"Who?" Raley looks at me and then down the table where I'm looking. "David? Yes, he's a bit of an odd one. Knitting. He's knitting. That's what he does all the time. It's a strange sort of thing for a boy to be doing, but no worse than poetry, I suppose." Raley takes another swig from his flask. "That day we met you at the station," he says, "David had been up to London to order some special sort of wool he's been wanting. That's how he spent his day off. Buying wool for his knitting."

"What's he knitting?"

Raley shrugs. "Don't think I've ever cared enough to ask," he says. "Knitting tends to rank right up there with dancing for me."

I lean my head on my hands. Candles have been lit and placed on the tables and the flickering light makes the white-chalk stars on the blackout curtains shimmer as though they were real. I think of Mrs. Woolf and that night I followed her through Tavistock Square. Now that she is dead, I am more sure than ever that it was really her. There were stars that night, I remember that, remember that first she looked up and then I did and there were stars above us.

"Those roses," I say to Raley. "The ones you saw in my room. The ones on fire. What colour were they?"

"White."

I think of one of the letters I was writing in my head to Mrs. Woolf. *Stars a white lace above the courtyard.* "Yes," I say. "A white lace."

Raley looks at me strangely. "What lace?" he says.

27

I can't sleep. After the dance is over and the men have straggled back up the hill to their house, I help the girls tidy the dining room. Everyone has had a good time. Golden Wonder is still having hers, out there in the dark saying good night to the soldier she's sweet on. I think it was her I originally discovered with the soldier in the barn. I try not to think of this, of where she and her soldier might be now, as I make my exit. The others are still laughing and joking, taking their time pushing the tables back in place, emptying the ashtrays. They are weary with exhilaration, and I leave them to it, to each other, and go back to my room.

Tonight nothing will work to ease me into sleep. I lie under *The Genus Rosa* but am merely irritated by the weight of it. It must have felt like this to Ellen Willmott sometimes, I think, at least metaphorically, all those years she spent working on it. How oppressively heavy it became.

I try to read some of *To the Lighthouse*, but the words sink out of sight the moment I say them in my head, cannot buoy me up as they used to.

From my bed, I look out the window at the night. I sleep with my curtains open now, even though I know I shouldn't. But the war isn't here the way it was in

London. There are barely any sounds of war, any evidence. It is hard to believe in the necessity of keeping one's curtains drawn.

There's a moon tonight. I can see the faint cast of its light over the quadrangle. Is Raley lying in bed looking out of his window at this same moon? I can still feel the residue of alcohol in my body, its heat moving in my veins. I feel riven with desire.

I get out of bed, dress hastily, and run down the stairs and out into the night. If I can't sleep, I might as well do something useful. I will go over to the walled garden and stand guard in case the chicken-thieving spirit dares to show up again. I am suddenly revived, seized with purpose, rushing through the cool night air, over the grass of the quadrangle. I am once more a woman of action. I hurtle myself willingly forward to my fate.

My fate is to crouch next to the old gardener's office in the kitchen garden, wishing I'd brought something to sit on because the ground is so cold. I lean up against the rough skin of bricks, peer out across the dark patch of dug earth towards the chicken coop. I can make out the shape of it. The moon sheds enough light so that I will be able to see anything or anyone approaching the enclosure. I wrap my arms around my knees and wait.

I remember being a child and sitting outside the house in the dark. The flowers in the beds were shadowy beside me, swaying slightly in a way I was used to, a way I found comforting. I was hiding from my mother, waiting for her to discover my absence and come looking for me. Eventually the ground would get too cold and hard and I would go back inside the house to find my mother asleep in her chair, or worse, reading a magazine. "Where did you come from?" she'd say.

I wasn't there when my mother died. I was due to visit her in the hospital that evening but I'd stayed late in my office, working on my notes. My mother died alone. The hospital telephoned me at the Royal Horticultural Society just as I was putting on my coat, to tell me that she'd died, and that she'd been asking for me. I didn't go to the hospital right away. There seemed no point. Instead I walked to Russell Square and sat on a bench near to the flowers. I sat there until someone found me and asked me if I was all right. I had been shaking, and a man walking by the bench had thought I was cold. "You should go home," he had said, and he'd touched me lightly on the shoulder, as if he knew me.

Now, sitting here in the dark of Mosel, my back cold from pressing into the garden wall, I wish I'd been there for my mother when she died. Once, a few days before that, she'd asked me to tell her the names of the roses in *The Genus Rosa*. I couldn't be bothered to lug the heavy books over from my office. But I wish I had. I could have done that, on her last night. I could have held her hand and whispered the names of the roses to her, amid the hospital clatter of her dying.

I am awakened by a noise from outside the garden wall. I wasn't aware of falling asleep. Have I dreamed my mother? There's the clatter again. I leap to my feet, hurl open the garden door, and rush out.

It's Jane. She's sitting on the black horse, reins in hand. I have startled them by bursting out of the garden. The horse flares sideways off the path.

"Gwen," says Jane, bringing the horse back under control. "What are you doing?"

I am suddenly at Mosel. This isn't the hospital. My mother is dead. "I'm trying to catch the chicken thief," I say, remembering. "It's not you, is it?"

"Gwen." Jane hops down from the horse, stands beside me on the path. "Of course it's not me. What would I want with a chicken?"

"Well," I say. "What are you doing with the horse?"

"I can't sleep. This is what I do at nights. I ride the horse over the fields. He gets exercised. I have something to occupy me. It's mutually beneficial." Jane puts a hand out and strokes the neck of the horse to calm him. I remember how easy they have always seemed together. And then I remember something else.

"I've seen you," I say. "From my window at night, racing across the quadrangle to the stables." That mysterious figure that I was on the verge of deciding was a ghost has been Jane on her way to ride the black horse.

"Yes," she says. "That was me."

"But you must sleep?"

"A little bit, at the end of the night. Often, after we ride, I just sleep in the stable. There's not much time between rubbing him down and then getting up to milk the cows." Jane leans back against the horse. "I haven't really slept since Andrew disappeared," she says. "I can't rest properly. Not until he comes home."

The night is cool around us. The horse is restless to be moving. He clatters his hooves on the stones of the path. That was the noise I heard from inside the garden.

"I'll walk you down to the fields," I say, and we walk down towards the South Garden. I had originally planned to plant the South Garden for potatoes, to utilize all the available agricultural potential of Mosel. But the truth is that I prefer the mix of grasses and flowers, the froth of blossom in the cherry trees. I don't want to ruin an aesthetic in favour of the bland practicality of planting potatoes. I have failed the spirit of the war effort. On bad days I chastise myself for this, but now, as we pass with the horse under the fragrant bower of the trees, I think there is no better choice I have made while here.

"What about David?" I ask, because I am confused by Jane's relationship with him. They seem so intimate. They seem as though they are falling in love.

"David?" Jane stops. We are at the edge of the fields. They fall away from us like the sea, awash with moonlight and their own dark vastness. "David is engaged to be married. He's entirely faithful."

And suddenly I can see how they have formed an alliance fuelled by their individual fidelities. It is not uncharged by attraction or desire, but it is tempered and controlled by these strict outside loyalties. How hard that must be to balance properly. How hard not to fall into the temptation of affection to hand, affection that's tangible. "You love Andrew," I say. I understand it so fully at this moment that I can almost feel it myself.

"It's all I have. Isn't it?" Jane puts her foot in the stirrup, swings herself back onto the horse. "How I treat it. How I serve it. My word. My heart. That's all I have." She pushes her heels against the flanks of the horse and they move away, out into the ocean of night. I can hear them long after I can see them. I watch them until they are gone.

28

After the midnight walk with Jane through the South Garden I make an authoritative decision. At breakfast the next morning I bring the plan of the estate, unroll it in the middle of the table, weighing the sides down with teapots, the toast rack, the pot of jam. "Right," I say with much conviction. I look around the table at my willing accomplices and see the dread on their faces.

"Oh, what?" says Salad Blue. I ignore her petulance. She has become decidedly bad-humoured lately, Evelyn. Yesterday she even snapped at British Queen for looking at her too often during dinner.

"I just have an idea," I say, by way of reassuring them. But it doesn't seem to make any difference to their attitude.

"You had an idea before," says Golden Wonder. To the girls, the chickens have become an example of failure, since they keep diminishing in number and the hens remaining are too traumatized by their missing sisters to lay properly.

But I am not to be silenced by their disapproval. I have thought about my idea, walking back from the South Garden last night, and I am sure it is a good one. I am sure it is the right one.

"Look," I say. "This is a map of the estate grounds

from 1900. As you can see, the gardens were much more elaborate and extensive then. They have shrunk considerably since that time. All I am proposing is that we restore some of that splendour, that instead of merely waiting for our harvest and the work of that, we put our energies into giving Mosel back some of its grace and grandeur."

No one says anything for a moment or two, but they are all looking at the estate plan, heads bent over the unrolled piece of paper. "What's this?" says Alice finally. She has her finger on one of the dotted lines on the lawn bordering the South Garden.

"That was the plan for a water garden," I say. "And this—" I point to the other area defined by a dotted outline. "This was going to be a maze."

"Oh, I like a maze," says Alice.

And that is what sways them over to my side, the idea of the maze. I'll never understand anyone, I think, as they're all talking excitedly about the non-existent maze. But it doesn't really matter. What matters is that the girls are supporting my idea, and the fact is that I cannot make my idea happen without their support.

Jane hasn't said anything during the whole episode. She seems distracted this morning, and now that I know her nocturnal habits, I also think she looks tired out. "What do you think?" I ask her. "Of my idea to restore the gardens?" I give her the gist of my idea in case she hasn't been listening to me.

"Yes," she says, pouring herself more tea and inadvertently rolling up a portion of the orchard. "Flowers instead of potatoes. I can see how that will be a good substitute."

And even though she is giving her support, I feel quite dispirited by her comment. Perhaps she is right and it is merely a choice between one thing or another, one diversion or another. Perhaps there is no real difference and every activity is just a way of filling time while we wait to return to our altered, and perhaps unrecognizable, lives. But it is hard to keep living like this, to keep thinking this way.

"What else can we do?" I say.

Jane unrolls the orchard and puts the teapot back among the apple trees. "Nothing," she says.

The girls are surprisingly eager to be once more working with a purpose. I think they are secretly relieved not to be mouldering out in the sun for yet another day. They set off optimistically with pruning shears and secateurs. Doris sharpens the blades of the mowing machine very efficiently with a whetstone and happily pushes it over the unruly grass of the quadrangle.

At mid-morning I go into the kitchen to make them some tea, carry it out to the lawn behind the dining hall. There is a moment, just before I call out that the tea's ready, when I stand on the lawn in the warm May sunshine, look down to where three of the girls are good-naturedly arguing about how much to clip off one of the giant yews by the path—there is a moment when I think of the last scene of *To the Lighthouse.* Lily Briscoe is standing on the lawn, painting the picture she'd first started ten years previous, feeling the past coalesce into the present and become a moment she can fully inhabit. The girls laugh from down the garden. I step onto the lawn, carrying the tea tray. The sun is clean on my bones. This is my life, I think. I'm not waiting for anything.

29

David starts coming down from the big house to spend the evenings with us. He says it gets too noisy up there, after dinner, when the men play loud, boisterous games and he just wants to be quiet. He usually arrives after the news broadcast, with his knitting tucked under his arm. He comes into the room that has the wireless and the chalked-on blackout curtains and sits in a chair by one of two lamps. The others usually disperse after the broadcast, except for Jane, who sits beside David while he knits, talking to him. He is making a sweater for his girlfriend. This is what he does—knits sweaters for her and sends them home.

"How many sweaters does she need?" I ask Jane. But I can see how this is a good way to remember someone and that David's need to make something for his girlfriend probably corresponds with her need to receive something from him, from this world unknown to her.

On the third or fourth evening that David is here, I am in my room, writing out notes for the restoration of the gardens, when there's a knock on my door. It's Jane. She's a little flushed from having run up the staircase.

"Gwen," she says. "I've decided to read to David while he knits. Do you have a book?"

"I have lots of books," I say. "What kind of book are you looking for?"

Jane leans against the door frame, considering and catching her breath. "Give me something *you* like," she says.

And so, in the evenings now, when the others have left the wireless room, Jane reads *To the Lighthouse* to David, while he sits in the chair by the lamp, knitting a sweater for his girlfriend. I am embarrassed to say that most nights I listen at the door. I didn't mean to, I was just passing by one night and heard Jane's voice reading those words I know so well and love so much. I had never heard anyone read Mrs. Woolf's words and I just pressed my forehead against the door and listened. I couldn't help myself. No one has ever read to me before. And the thing is, I'm sure that Jane wouldn't even mind if I went into the room and sat there to listen. But she isn't reading to me, and I don't feel right doing that. So I stand at the door, leaning into the wood and almost forgetting to breathe, I am listening so intently.

Jane has a lovely reading voice. It is melodic and, unlike anything else about her, it is slow and measured. She reads as though there were all the time in the world to tell the story. And when I hear that voice polishing those words so that they shine inside me, I miss my old life—London, my mother—so acutely that some nights I actually cry. I haven't read *To the Lighthouse* in so long, but I remember it all. I listen again, to the tale of the Ramsay family who are spending their summer at a house in what is meant to be the Hebrides but which I know from the flora really isn't. The family are joined for the summer by several guests, including the painter, Lily Briscoe. The story concerns a thwarted expedition to sail to a lighthouse to visit the lighthouse keeper and his son.

Before, when I'd read the book, I liked the character of Mrs. Ramsay, but now, hearing Jane read it from behind the door, I find her pessimistic self-centredness very unsympathetic. Her great gift is that she responds to life, lives in the moment. She is spontaneous and enthusiastic, gets swept up with what is happening. Most of the other characters aren't capable of this and so they are drawn to her. But she often connects to people emotionally by feeling sorry for them. I don't approve of this at all because I am always suspecting people of this in relation to me. And yet Lily has laid her head on Mrs. Ramsay's lap, has wanted her to be a sanctuary, as everyone else has.

Jane is reading the part where Mr. Ramsay, who is always pacing up and down on the terrace, reciting *The Charge of the Light Brigade*, looks out across the bay and compares himself to a sand dune. Later, his friend William Bankes will compare their friendship to the same sand dune. *The Charge of the Light Brigade* is a poem that pays tribute to a cavalry division that charged the wrong way.

I close my eyes and lean my head against the door. I can smell the wood and the mustiness of the hallway. There is no sound but Jane's voice from inside the room, beating the air with words.

30

There are only two stories left to be drawn onto the blackout curtains in the wireless room. Mine and Jane's. Despite much pleading and coercion, Jane has stuck to her refusal to tell a story. "I just like it as it is," she will say to repeated requests for her to take the chalk in hand and fill in her allotted segment of curtain. "I like it black." And there is no convincing her otherwise, although we do tell her pointedly that we will just leave her space blank until she changes her mind.

I have debated about the filling in of my particular space on the curtain. There I am, a vertical rectangle next to the Lumper's piece of music. The black of the drapes seems so funereal that, at first, I think I should use the space to do some sort of memorial to my mother, or to London. But although I did love both my mother and the city I lived in, I no longer suffer any illusions that I was loved much in return. So I fill my space with what has responded positively to my love. Flowers. I fill the space with flowers. I pin them onto the fabric and make a garden. And because I don't want to be limited only to flowers that will dry well, I change what is pinned to the curtain almost daily. Some days I make a garden for colour—say, a garden of yellow with dahlias and lilies, snapdragons and yellow geums. I make a garden just of variegated leaves and a garden that is long, trailing tendrils of ivy. Inspired by the lost garden, I sometimes make gardens to a specific theme and then have the girls try to guess what it is I'm attempting to show. I fashion a garden just of plants used for medicinal purposes. I make a garden of flowers beginning with the letter *M*. I try to get it all done in the afternoon, so that when the girls come down after supper to listen to the wireless, it is a surprise. And just as their enthusiasm for the maze on the estate plan made me realize how much closer to children than adults the girls really are, it is much the same with the blackout-curtain garden. They love seeing the new arrangement. They love having to guess at the mystery I've created for them to solve. They are so easy, these girls. It's just a question of working with them rather than against them. It's so much simpler than it was at the beginning of our acquaintanceship.

Today I'm pinning a clutch of irises to the curtain. I am making a garden of flowers that are also women's names. I hear a noise behind me and turn around to see Evelyn in the doorway. "Oh," she says, embarrassed that I've caught her here well before time. "It's only me. I've been thinking of this all day. I just couldn't wait until after supper."

They were never the enemy, these girls at Mosel. If I had been more generous when I first arrived here, instead of being so defensive about my deficiencies, I would have seen this sooner. They weren't unwilling to like me. I just never gave them the proper chance to do it on their terms.

"Well, now that you're here," I say, "why don't you come and help me pin these up."

31

The Lumper's father comes to see me. He shows up one day after breakfast, waiting outside the walled garden, cap in hand. He is a big man, in his middle forties, with the rough, weathered skin of someone who has spent his life working outdoors.

"Miss Davis?" he says. He looks nervous. "Doris said I'd be finding you here."

I wonder how Doris has described me to him. I offer him my hand. "I'm pleased to meet you, Mr. Frant," I say. "Thank you for coming to see me."

"It's a pleasure, ma'am. Good to be able to have a look at the old place again."

"Well, come on, then. Let me show you around properly." I take him through the kitchen garden first, show him the neatly humped earth under which the potatoes slumber, the stakes for the runner beans. He makes no comment on this labour, but when he sees the chickens out in their run, pecking disconsolately at their kitchen scraps, he stops walking.

"Oh," he says. "Chickens are not a good idea. There's a ghost what takes them in the night."

"Even when you were working here?" For that is almost twenty-five years ago.

"Oh, yes." Mr. Frant twists his cap in his hands. Instead of smoking, I think. He wants to have a cigarette but thinks it might be bad manners. "I never saw it, mind you. But several of the others did."

"Well, never mind about the ghost," I say. Really, I am a little sick of the whole chicken-thieving-spectre spectacle. I've a good mind to have the whole lot slaughtered and made into *coq au vin* by Victualette Noir. I lead Mr. Frant away from the chicken run and steer him towards the small brick gardener's office. I open the door and let him peer inside.

"Mr. Thoby's office," he says. "It was always very tidy. Everything in its proper place. Mr. Thoby was a bit of a stickler for order."

I go into the office and remove the gardener's ledger from the desk drawer. I take it back outside to Mr. Frant and open it to the list of names in the front of the book. "Do you remember these men?" I ask him.

Doris's father poises his hand over the list of names and I notice how his hand shakes. He hadn't been twisting his cap in his hands. His hands had been shaking. "Of course," he says, and puts his finger down onto one of the names. "Look, there I am." And there he is—Lewis Frant. "I was one of the labourers, that's why I'm near the bottom." He moves his finger up the row of names. "Foreman at the top. Then the five gardeners. Then two under-gardeners. The rest of us were labourers, though some had more knowledge of horticulture than others."

"Will you walk with me?" I tuck the ledger under my arm and lead Mr. Frant out of the walled garden. I walk him along the path and across the lawn to the South

Garden. He keeps looking around, pointing out where trees used to be that must have met with disease or fallen down in a storm. Wandering with him over these grounds that are now so familiar to me is like imposing an imaginary landscape over a real one. A similar experience, in many ways, to my reading of the estate plan.

When we get to the South Garden we walk among the cherry trees. They have all dropped their blossoms now, a spray of pink covers the grass. Mr. Frant stops at the edge of the field, looks out across the vast sweep of land. "This place has not changed," he says. Perhaps because the meadow is planted with bulbs and the trees need little managing, this garden that is half wild and half cultivated has managed to survive as it was. Its balance has saved it. Anything too wild would have grown rampant. Anything too cultivated quickly would have lost its civilized form.

I take Mr. Frant to the orchard. He runs his hand along the limbs of the espaliered fruit trees on the wall. His hand moves across the limbs as though they were rungs on a ladder. "I never liked the look of this," he says. "Unnatural, that's what it is."

"You worked in the orchard?"

"Sometimes. We were rotated around the grounds, but there were some who worked better in certain places."

"Who worked here more than the others?" The orchard is the closest area to the hidden garden, and because of the various connections between the flowers growing in it and the fruit growing here, I believe there to be a connection between whoever worked in the orchard and whoever made the hidden garden. I believe they could be the same person.

Mr. Frant pushes his hand through his hair. "We were lads, weren't we?" he says. I don't answer. They would have been boys near to twenty years old, the garden labourers on this estate. They would have been the same age as the girls here now. "There were three who were in this orchard more than the others. One under-gardener and two labourers."

I open the ledger to the list of names at the front of the book. "Who were they?"

Lewis Frant touches the three names lightly, the way he ran his hand along the limbs of the espaliered trees. "Thomas Walton. Samuel Hood. William Allen."

"Did anything unusual or particularly noteworthy ever happen in the orchard?" I ask.

"What sort of thing?" He looks confused by my question. *Love*, I want to say. Was this a place where lovers met? Was this the place that inspired the hidden garden? Whatever happened here fuelled the planting of those coded flowers, the writing of those words on the pieces of metal and stone. I am sure of that.

"Anything," I say. "Anything out of the ordinary. Even anything ordinary."

Lewis Frant stands very still under the apple trees. "We were lads, weren't we?" he says again.

I wish I could see what he sees as he looks back over twenty-five years, back to when he was a boy working here among a whole staff of boys, back to when this orchard would have been properly managed, when the whole of Mosel would have looked easily magnificent in the way that is possible when so much effort is being made to make everything appear effortless, appear completely natural. Back to a time before the wars.

"No," says Lewis Frant. "I don't remember anything of note ever happening in the orchard. But I wasn't down here enough to really know. I was mostly set to work on the lawns and on the beds around the quadrangle. They're completely ruined now, aren't they, ma'am? I was having a look before I came to wait for you." Lewis Frant twists his cap through his shaking hands again. "That's where I used to be," he says. "I remember that area of the estate very well. Would you like to know who worked with me there?"

"No, that won't be necessary." I feel defeated. I'm convinced that something important did happen in the orchard, but Lewis Frant is my only connection to that possibility and he is turning out to be as disappointing a witness to history as the fruit trees themselves.

"I was the only one of us who didn't go," says Lewis Frant.

"Didn't go?"

"To the war. All the other lads went off when they were called, but I have a touch of the palsy." He holds out his hands in front of him to demonstrate and I see the shiver in them. "Aggravated by nerves," he says. "Not a useful thing in a nervous situation such as war." He lowers his arms. "What's that?" He's looking over the stone wall and has spotted the top half of the topiary angel.

"Oh, that," I say. "One of the girls had a go with the shears, just to see what she could do."

Lewis Frant just stares at the green angel. "Well," he says. "That's something I'd forgotten."

"What?"

"There used to be something else there. Not an angel,

but something. One of those yews was cut into some kind of a shape." He frowns, trying to bring the memory back.

Anything in that spot would have been to mark the entrance to the hidden garden, I think—one of the yews clipped into a shape. A reminder of where the entrance was? A signal for someone else to find it?

"What?" I say. "What was it?"

"An animal," says Lewis Frant. "Yes, that's it. One of those big yews was carved into the head of an animal. A fox. It was the head of a fox."

After Lewis Frant has walked out of the orchard, back towards the quadrangle and the buildings to visit his daughter, I go past the green angel, squeeze through the yew hedge, and enter the hidden garden. I was tempted to show it to Lewis Frant, but I resisted, reasoning that if he knew of its existence, he would have mentioned it.

I sit on the bench by the edge of the garden and open the head gardener's ledger. Mr. Thoby, I think. It's Mr. Thoby's record of his garden. I look at the list of names at the front of the book and then flip to the last entry, the one made in 1916 when the gardens were essentially shut down. Thomas Walton, Samuel Hood, and William Allen all have lines drawn through their names. Straight, unwavering lines. All three men were killed in the war.

32

The last garden in the trilogy of gardens blooms fully in June. It is the Garden of Faith and it consists of only one thing. An enormous, tangled wash of white rose. Now it completely engulfs a bower fashioned together, much like my rustic bench, out of sticks and branches. At one time the rose must have been sweetly woven through the wood and there would have been a nice balance between the tumbling white blooms and the clean, straight lines of the sticks. Now the rose has completely taken over its support and one side of the bower has collapsed under the weight of blossom and vine.

I don't interfere with the rose. I don't trim it or tie it up or stake it along the contours of the bower. I cut a few of the blooms off to pin to my section of the black-out curtain in the wireless room, but that is all. After I scrabbled around in the earth beneath the bower and found the name for this portion of the garden on a stone, I decided that Faith should be left to find its own way.

The rose is called 'Madame Hardy.' It is a Damask Rose, with large, double blooms that are often as wide across as the span of a hand. It has a very strong, haunting fragrance, with a hint of lemon under the musk of perfume. Though a shrub rose, it is tall and can be used as a climber, as it has been here in the hidden garden. A distinctive feature of this beautiful rose is the small, emerald-green eye in the centre of the bloom. Bred by Eugene Hardy at the Luxembourg Gardens in France in 1832, it was named after his wife. In a twist of irony it is not a very "hardy" rose, often needing to be staked and supported, easily damaged by wind and rain. Perhaps this is why it was entwined around the bower.

I sit on the bench in the sun and look at the flurry of white, anchoring one end of the garden. Why this rose and not another? I look out over the flower bed, beyond to the woods, the thin spires of trees rising into the blue and promised heaven. I don't know what to think any more. I had been hoping that Doris's father would have some answers, but the only interesting and vaguely useful piece of information he had to relay was about the yew in front of this garden being cut into the shape of a fox. And I still don't know to what purpose.

The sun glints off the pure white of the roses. 'Madame Hardy,' I think. Thomas Hardy. Thomas Walton, the name of the under-gardener whom Lewis Frant remembered working often in the orchard. But I have lost the thread of this garden. I have not found it in its original language. I have discovered it in a foreign script and I have tried to translate it so that it makes sense to me, in this world, but it won't come down to me. The past won't come down to me as I sit in the middle of this bright June afternoon in 1941. The past is a language I don't know how to read or answer.

33

Jane has almost finished reading *To the Lighthouse* to David. I can't bear the story to be over. I'm down there every night now, outside the room where they sit, my ear pressed to the closed door. I don't know what David thinks of Virginia Woolf for he never says anything I can hear. There's just the click of his knitting needles underneath the smooth rhythm of Jane's reading voice, like the noise of a small machine or a cricket in the dusk.

I am hanging on to everything now, every scene, every word. I hear the pause Jane makes at the end of a page and I experience such a sense of loss I almost cry out. Goodbye to Mrs. Ramsay, and to Lily Briscoe on the lawn. Goodbye to the boat finally sailing to the lighthouse with Mr. Ramsay and his two youngest children. The wind has just dropped and the children are watching the evidence of this in the sails of the boat. Their feelings are slowing with the momentum of the boat. Mr. Ramsay, oblivious to this, is reading a book.

I lean my head against the door and it moves open a crack. I can see Jane reading to David, how she sits close beside him, her head bent over the sweater he is fashioning from his skeins of wool.

There is Lily Briscoe on the lawn, trying to finish her

painting, looking up from her easel to a memory of Mrs. Ramsay on the steps of the house with James. Her hand holds a paintbrush as a conductor holds a baton. This is the music of the moment, these words and images, and all of a sudden I know that it doesn't matter whether or not it was Mrs. Woolf I followed through London that June evening seven years ago. I will never be closer to her than now. The book is the shared experience, the shared intimacy. There is Virginia Woolf, dipping her pen in ink, looking up from the page with Lily on the lawn, to the view from her window. Here am I, looking across the room to the summer dark beating against these mullioned panes. There is Jane reading the words aloud to a young soldier sitting beside her. It is a place we have all arrived at, this book. The characters fixed on the page. The author who is only ever writing the book, not gardening or walking or talking, and while the reader is reading, the author is always here, writing. The author is at one end of the experience of writing and the reader is at the other, and the book is the contract between you. And this is what you're doing, being in the book, entering it as one enters a room and sees there, through the French doors to the garden, Lily Briscoe painting on the lawn.

When a writer writes, it's as if she holds the sides of her chest apart, exposes her beating heart. And even though everything wants to heal, to close over and protect the heart, the writer must keep it bare, exposed. And in doing this, all of life is kept back, all the petty demands of the day-to-day. The heart is a river. The act of writing is the moving water that holds the banks apart, keeps the muscle of words flexing so that the reader can be carried along by this movement. To be given space and the chance to leave one's earthly world. Is there any greater freedom than this?

I wipe my hand across my face. I am crying. I don't want to sniffle in case I am heard. I lean my head into the door and it opens an inch wider.

The story is over. Jane closes the book. She had been reading more slowly as she approached the last scene, as though she didn't want to leave the book either. She doesn't say anything, just closes the book and holds it in her lap, still looking down at it.

I should leave, but I can't move from the doorway. I feel rooted here.

David lays down his needles. "That was nice," he says. And then, "I'm out of wool. I should go back up to the house."

Jane raises her head. "Here," she says. "Use this." And she takes off her jumper with one fluid movement and hands it to David.

It's as if I've never seen Jane before, never known her. With just an undervest on, she looks unbelievably thin. Arms no wider around than the sticks of the bower. A collarbone protruding from the skin in all its detail. And with that one gesture I learn the fundamental truth of her. When she takes off her sweater and, without thinking, hands it over to David to use as wool, I can see how Jane loves. And I know—with all my heart I know—that there is no protection in the world for someone who loves like that.

34

The chickens are disappearing at the rate of about one per week. There are now only three left in the coop, only three chances to discover what is happening to them. I am determined to solve this mystery, and start spending every night in the walled garden. I bring out a cushion from one of the chairs in the wireless room, and a blanket for the colder nights, and I make myself a sort of nest positioned between the wall of the garden and one of the walls of Mr. Thoby's office. I bring a Thermos of tea and a battery-powered torch in case I need to surprise and apprehend the culprit, although I get so stiff from sitting on the ground all night that I would have trouble springing to my feet and surging dramatically across the garden in pursuit of the thief. I am not proud to say that periodically I have fallen asleep while on watch, but that, luckily, nothing untoward has occurred while I've been snoring against the bricks.

It is now the third night of my vigil. The moon is high and bright. I will not even need my torch if an intruder arrives tonight. I can see clearly all the way across the garden to where the chickens are no doubt cowering in fright in their straw beds.

I have told only Jane of my plan. The past two nights

I have heard her clatter by on the horse on the way to ride across the darkened fields. I have to admit that last night, when she rode by the garden, returning to the stables in the very early morning, the noise of the horse on the stones woke me up.

If only I could read while out here, then I'd be less likely to fall asleep. It's the boredom of remaining motionless for so many hours in a row that sabotages me.

Tonight I am restless. I can't seem to get comfortable in my makeshift burrow. I wriggle around on the cushion, wrap the blanket around me, rip it off. I want to drink the tea, just for the sheer relief of having something to do, but I'm afraid to do this too early because of the lavatory problem—the fact that there isn't one out here and at a certain point in the night it becomes a problem.

I stare over the moonlit garden to the chicken run and try to will something to happen, but it doesn't work—all is as inert as ever.

I am so ridden by the tedium of my task that the moment I hear the sound of the horse outside the walls of the garden I lurch to my feet and rush through the door. Jane is just riding slowly past. "Wait," I say, running beside the horse to keep pace with her. "Where are you going?"

Jane reins up and the horse stops his forward gait. "You know where I'm going," she says.

"Wouldn't you like some tea first?" I have nothing else to offer, and often by the time I actually get around to drinking the tea, it's already cold.

Jane grins at me. "A little bored, are you?" she says.

"No ghosts to keep you company?" She swings down from the horse. "All right," she says. "I'll come and sit with you for a little while." She leads the horse off the path and wraps his reins around a tree close to the lawn.

"You have the cushion," I say, once I've lured her inside the walled garden. But she's so small that my act of generosity is unnecessary. There's room for both of us to perch on the square of padded green.

Jane looks out over the earth of the beds. "It looks quite nice at night," she says. She turns to me. "What about that tea, then?"

I pour her tea into the one cup I've brought and I use the metal top of the Thermos for myself. We sit on the cushion, in the dark garden, sipping our tea. I am so grateful to have company that I keep forgetting I am on a vigil, keep wanting to talk the silence away.

"Shush," Jane keeps saying. "We're waiting for the ghost."

After a little while I calm down, am able to sit quietly and watch. Jane calms me down. I thought that when I listened to her read through the door of the wireless room. How calm and steady her voice was as she read Virginia Woolf to David. How her reading voice was like a cool hand laid against my burning forehead. I want to tell her that I heard her read, but I don't know how much she would mind my spying on her and David, for this is how it could be perceived, as nothing more than spying.

"Why don't you eat?" I say instead, for I am remembering the thinness of her body when she pulled her sweater over her head. And when I thought about it later, I realized that I'd never actually seen her eat a full meal. She always had an excuse to push the dinner plate away from her.

Jane looks at me. "Don't," she says. "I eat enough to stay alive. That's all that matters, isn't it?"

She has no margin of safety around her. I saw that very clearly the night she handed her sweater to David. No protection. I suddenly feel afraid for her. "What if Andrew doesn't come back?" I say.

There's a noise from outside the garden. A squeal from the horse, as though he's been startled. Something white flashes in front of the chicken coop, leaps over the fence of the run. I am too surprised to surge to my feet as planned. It has all happened so fast I can't be sure of what I've seen. Jane has grabbed my hand, and we watch as the white figure reappears from the coop, a chicken fluttering in panic from between its jaws. The ghost of Mosel is an albino fox. Having cleared the fence, it dashes off to the side, and disappears through what must be a hole in the wall.

I look at Jane. She looks at me. She hasn't let go of my hand. "That was so expertly done," she says. I think of what Lewis Frant remembered, how one of the yews marking my hidden garden had been clipped into the shape of a fox. Perhaps there have always been these albino foxes on the grounds of Mosel. And probably Jane and I aren't the first to sit out here in the walled garden, waiting for the ghost to show up. I'm beginning to feel as though everything has happened before, that our story has already been told. Just as we were powerless to stop the fox stealing the chicken, so there seems to be an inevitability to all that takes place at Mosel. This is a ghost story. And we have somehow become the ghosts of these young men who worked this estate before the Great War. The living are the dead.

"Gwen," says Jane. "What's the matter? You look as if you've just seen a fox."

That dissolves it. The patina of present over past lifts and it is just now. I am here in the garden, in the dark, with Jane beside me. The furrowed earth looks wet with moonlight. I let go of her hand. "Yes," I say. "That was so expertly done."

35

The work on the grounds progresses nicely. By the end of June they are beginning to resemble themselves again. The weather, though a little cool at night, is good enough that we decide to have one of the dances with the soldiers outside on the lawn behind the dining hall.

There is a great discussion about light for this dance. The girls want to stud the lawn with torches, for romantic atmosphere, but because of the war we are not supposed to have any light outside at night.

"But the war never comes here," says Golden Wonder, when I remind them of the light restrictions we are meant to be obeying. "Adolf is busy invading Russia. Couldn't we just put the torches out if we hear a plane?" She is involved in a serious romance with one of the Canadian soldiers and wants everything to look as nice as possible when the men come for the dance.

It is now easy for us to ignore the war. Our work on the estate has shifted from war effort to restoration. We live at Mosel as though it is where we really live, not merely where we are posted. And Golden Wonder is right, the war is distant here. The war is the nightly radio broadcast, and sometimes, lately, we've even been turning this off before it's finished. We have been, mistakenly as it turns out, believing that the war has become a choice and we can simply choose not to participate if we feel like it.

So I agree to the torches and Golden Wonder's rather idiotic suggestion of extinguishing them at the first hint of bombers overhead. For my own peace of mind, I do insist on only half the number of torches the girls had originally wanted. This pleases everyone, and the Women's Land Army spends ages making the torches and planting them in the lawn. I have to admit that, on the night of the dance, when they are all lit and glow like fireflies on the stretch of grass, there has never been anything more beautiful. After we light them we just stand there on the lawn, almost in shock, I think. It has been years since we have seen benign light at night. Years. The most ordinary event has become this extraordinary moment where we stand silently together on the lawn, watching the flames from the torches ignite the dark.

We hear the men come down the road from the house. The music from the Victrola spooling through the darkness. Evelyn and Alice and Golden Wonder, whose name is really Daphne, rush out to the road to meet them.

"Thank God no one from the higher-ups can see us

now," I say to Jane, who stands beside me on the lawn by one of our bright, illicit beacons of folly.

"Don't blame yourself," she says. "All societies sink into the mud of hedonism if you let them."

"Well, exactly," I say. I'm starting to feel guilty again, feel that I should have put a stop to everything before it got so out of hand. I look at Jane standing calmly beside me. If I said this to her, she would just tell me that I think I'm more powerful than I actually am. And isn't that it? I'm one of many, not one above many. "It's a mixed border," I say to Jane.

"What are you talking about?" Jane lights a cigarette. The men come around the corner of the building. Daphne is already dancing with her soldier. The man carrying the Victrola walks behind them. I see Raley near the end of the line and I feel ill.

"Get out your dance card," says Jane, and we move forward to greet the men.

36

Before the dance gets properly underway, while the girls are still fussing with the torches and the soldiers are fussing with the music, I stand off to the side of the grassy dance floor with David. He is smoking a cigarette. We are both watching Jane as she flits about, from torch to torch, with her box of matches.

"What happens to your jumpers?" I ask.

"What?" He looks puzzled.

"Your jumpers," I say. "The ones you knit."

"I send them home to my girlfriend." David stamps out his cigarette and reaches inside his jacket pocket. "She wears them in the places we used to go together. Her sister photographs her doing this and she sends me the picture." He pulls out a handful of small photographs, taps the top one. "That's her. That's Abby."

I look down at the image of a young, dark-haired girl standing on a large black rock.

"We used to row out there in the spring to look for birds' eggs." David taps the photograph again. "That was the best sweater I ever made. You can't tell from this, but it's the night sky from above that rock. The sweater I knitted in black, with bursts of white for the stars overhead. I even got the constellations right," he says.

If I peer hard at the photograph in David's hand, at the girl on the rock and the sweater on the girl, I can see stabs of white breaking open the black. I can see the stars he means. I can see too how their love works for them. How he makes a mystery for her to solve. How she sends back the proof.

"David!" Jane waves from across the lawn.

David grins at me, hastily re-pockets his photographs. "Duty calls," he says, and he bounds down the slope towards the waving figure of Jane.

The lawn behind the dining hall is low, slopes down towards the South Garden. As the night cools, the air becomes misty, cocoons of fog float above the grass. Several of the torches go out because of the damp and have to be relit.

Later, I stand with Raley in the same place I'd stood

with David. Couples appear suddenly out of the fog, then recede just as suddenly. The music announces then mourns them. "I saw the Mosel ghost," I say to Raley. "It was a white fox."

"Well done, Captain Davis." Raley drinks from his flask, forgetting to offer it to me. He has been distant all evening, just standing here watching the soldiers and the Land Girls dance.

I take the flask out of his hand and drink from it. He looks at me in surprise. "You forgot your manners," I say. And then it strikes me that he is the most well-mannered person I have ever met. Under all situations he has always been exceedingly polite. "What's the matter?" I pass the whisky back and he drinks from it again.

"We're to be posted," he says. "Tomorrow they're moving us to Sussex. From there we'll go into the war. I haven't told the men yet. Thought I'd give them one final carefree evening to enjoy themselves."

I watch the dancers spin through the fog. The glow of the torches behind them, like a candle someone has left burning in a window to wish them home. "Don't go," I say, but thankfully he doesn't hear me.

"Look at them," says Raley. "A year from today and we could all be dead. Doesn't it seem impossible to believe?"

A slight wind swirls the fog gently in front of us, as though it's being stirred. The wind is from the south. I can smell the sea. "Come with me," I say to Raley, and I take his hand and lead him away from the dance.

Even in the dark, with the moon slipping in and out from behind the clouds, I am able to find my way through the orchard and around the stone wall. The green angel looks sombre in the darkness, rising on its stalk of hedge. I'm not sure Raley even sees it, as I pull him through the gap in the yews.

The garden is all silvery with the mist and moonlight. It looks like something seen underwater, blurry and fluid. I still have Raley firmly by the hand, walk him around the perimeter of it. "This is a secret," I say. "No one knows it's here. It was planted by someone who worked at Mosel around 1916."

"What is it?" asks Raley.

"It's a garden of love." I guide him slowly from one end of it to the other. "This is Longing, much of it no longer in bloom. This is Loss." I stop in front of the wave of peonies, frozen in the act of crashing to the ground, of going overboard.

But Raley isn't looking at the Garden of Loss. He's looking ahead to where the roses glisten bright as stars at the end of the flower bed. "Those were in my dream," he says. "That night I was drunk and fell asleep in your room. They were burning above my head, and I swear they were still burning when I woke."

Again, as I did the other night with the fox, I feel as though we have fallen into spaces opened by the past. I feel that our story has already been told. Perhaps the person who made this garden had slept in my bedroom. Perhaps what Raley dreamt had actually happened there, or been thought about enough for it to slip through the wall of time into this reality. We are our own ghosts already, I think.

"I don't want to go, Gwen," says Raley. "I'm afraid."

I lead him to the bench and make him sit down. He leans his head down to my shoulder and I reach up with both arms and hold him while he cries. His head is heavy, full of rain. I touch his cheek, the strong bones around his eyes. I touch his lips, gently, so gently, and then I kiss him. I kiss him and he lets me. Then he kisses me back. We push against each other and topple off the bench onto the grass. I scrape my arm on the wood on the way down. I will have that scratch longer than I will have anyone, and in the weeks to come I will open it and open it, never let it heal, let the jagged seam of blood fill and fill, and empty.

Raley lies on top of me. His body is heavy and insistent. He kisses me and I feel as if I have never breathed before now. That all this time I was only dying. I wrap my arms around him, feel his ribs under his shirt, pull it up and run my hands over his skin, soft as petals. Don't go, I think, as I slide my fingers over each blunt thorn in his spine. Don't go. The moon moves out from behind a cloud and turns his blond hair white in the milky dark, in the thin milky dark. And then the wind stirs and I can smell the roses. I swear it is that, it is the scent of the night roses that makes me say what I feel but never meant to utter. It is the scent of roses, and I swear this has happened before. The roses have made this happen before. They are burning above me. Raley is burning above me. "I love you," I say.

I will think later, over and over again, that if only I hadn't said those words we would have been lovers that night. But my telling him I love him has made Raley stiffen and roll off me, lie on his back on the grass beside me with his hands up to his face. "Oh, Gwen," he says. "No." And then he sits up.

The feeling of him gone from my body is the loneliest I have ever been. And there will never be anything to relieve it. For one moment I was no longer empty. For one moment I was alive. Until I made the mistake of calling it love.

"I'm sorry," says Raley. "I'm truly sorry."

I can't get up. I lie on my back in the grass. I can feel the sting of the cut on my arm. "I'm not so bad in the dark. Am I?" I just say it, because it doesn't matter if I say the truth now.

Raley kneels beside me. "Gwen," he says, and he picks me up and holds me against his chest while I cry. "You're wrong about yourself. But I can't," he says. "It would be so unfair."

"But I don't care," I say, into the space between his collarbone and neck. I don't care. I don't care if he doesn't love me back. I don't care that he's leaving tomorrow. I just need him to lie on top of me again. This is all I need. But I'm crying too hard to get the words out.

"Gwen," says Raley. I can feel the tension in his body, can feel the sweat from his hands through my shirt. "My friend who died. Peter. He wasn't just my friend. He was my lover. We have been, had been, lovers since we were young. I've tried, while I've been here at Mosel, I've tried to get over it. But I can't. There is nothing else for me." Raley lets go of me and we look at each other across this great distance that has seemed to open between us. I remember the first time I went to see him at the house, how he was listening to the Mozart *Requiem.* I see how I have just been another attempt at comfort. Another sort of poultice.

"I'm sorry," he says, "I never meant to hurt you." He stands up.

I wipe my sleeve across my face to staunch the tears and struggle to my feet as well. Behind Raley I can see the mocking white of the roses. And just as I had always thought the garden was made to commemorate love between someone who worked at Mosel and someone from the village, between a man and a woman, now I see how that story could have been different too. Thomas or Samuel or William could have made that garden for one of the other gardeners on the estate, or for one another. Nothing is certain. Nothing is known. The roses burn white in the darkness behind us. White as ashes.

37

The soldiers leave the estate the next morning. We hear the engine of the car as it winds up and down the hill, ferrying the men to the train station. We sit at the table, long after breakfast is over, listening to this particular song play over and over again. There is a small, grim knot of us at breakfast. Daphne has not appeared this morning. Jane hasn't emerged from the barn. I think the rest of us are afraid to be alone, even though we're also having trouble speaking to each other. We just sit together in our uneasy assembly. It's so quiet in the dining hall that I can hear the birdsong from outside the windows.

It is Raley who comes to say goodbye. Most of the men have been taken to the train. He is the last to go. He comes to the door of the dining hall, a brown paper parcel in his hands. And even though I don't want to talk to him or see him, I can't stop myself from rushing over to him the moment he moves into the door frame. He is all turned out, all neat and trim in his uniform, hair slicked down, ready to go into war looking like the soldier he is supposed to be. Only when I am close to him and smell the familiar blossom of alcohol on his breath am I reassured that he is still himself.

"Hello, Captain Davis," he says. His voice is warm and charming as usual.

"Hello, Captain Raley."

He smiles at me, a slow, sad smile. " 'Never morning wore/ To evening, but some heart did break,' " he says. "It's from that infernal poem."

"I thought you'd gone off poetry."

"Poetry is a little slower to go off me." Raley reaches out and touches my cheek. "I did love that," he says. "That night I read to you from that infernal poem."

I almost start to cry, right there in the morning, in the dining hall with the cluster of girls behind me at the table. That night Raley offered me as compensation, I remember mostly as my mad scramble to find the plan of the estate. I was barely listening to him read to me. I think of how intently I have been listening at the door of the wireless room to Jane reading to David. I have missed my chance. There is no other way to say this. I have missed my chance at the closest thing likely to come my way under the category of love.

"Right," I say, because I can think of nothing else. But it is not right at all.

Raley takes his hand away from my face. He holds the parcel out to me. "Could you give this to Jane? David couldn't bring himself to come in person."

"Of course." I take the parcel. The paper crackles like fire as it passes between us. Raley's good manners brought him here to say goodbye. His good manners have translated, in this instance, into courage. "Good luck, then," I say.

"Thank you. I'm sure luck is what I'll be needing. Goodbye, Gwen." Raley lifts his hand and waves to the girls over my shoulder.

Don't go, I think, as he is turning in the doorway and going. I hear his shoes on the stone steps as he walks away from me. I stand there for a moment, the package for Jane in my hands, and then I run through the dining hall, run through the passage that connects to the west wing. I race along the corridor to my room, grab what I've come for, and fly down the staircase outside, past Mr. Frant's mixed border, through the arch, and out onto the driveway. The car with Raley in the passenger seat is just pulling away. "Wait!" I rush up, completely out of breath, and thrust the book into his hands. We don't speak. I am too out of breath from my frantic dash to say anything comprehensible. He looks at me with what I can only interpret as tenderness. My usual barrage of self-deprecating protectiveness surrenders completely before that look of his. He tucks my copy of *To the Lighthouse* inside his jacket. The car drives off. I stand on the driveway, long after the car is down the hill and gone. Past the stream and through the village. Long after it has turned into the entrance to the station. In some measure, I am always standing watching the car with Raley in it drive away. I am always there. Even now.

38

I leave the parcel for Jane in her room. I can't face anyone right now, even her. I just put the package down on her neatly made bed, sheets all crisped up straight, and I go outside, walk through the orchard to the lost garden. There is nowhere else for me to go.

What I've always found interesting in gardens is looking at what people choose to plant there. What they put in. What they leave out. One small choice and then another, and soon there is a mood, an atmosphere, a series of limitations, a world. I would not have chosen the same plants as the anonymous gardener if I were planting a garden of love, but there are some flowers we have in common. Peonies for loss. I too would choose the breaking wave of peonies for loss.

I sit on the bench, facing the garden. I have sat here for so many hours. I have looked and looked at this one patch of planted ground, trying to figure out what it meant, trying to break the code. But in searching for the story I have also made my own story here. This is my garden now.

It is a low, cloudy morning, this one which the soldiers have left us at Mosel. The air is warm and humid, noisy with insects and birdsong.

In the end I will have to make a choice about how to tell my story. And I will have to make a choice about how to tell the story of the person who made this garden, and the garden itself. There has to be a moment of going forward, when all the possibilities are left behind.

This is what I have made of the story of the garden. I think someone was in love with Thomas Walton. Perhaps someone from outside Mosel, but more likely someone who worked on the estate. It could have been one of the women who worked in the kitchen. It could have been a maid from the house. It could even have been the mistress of the estate herself. It could also have been one of the other gardeners. Perhaps Samuel Hood or William Allen. Whoever was the lover, the love itself was fuelled by something that happened in the orchard. Something very powerful. A moment of recognition that would alter a life.

I look at the heads of the peonies, fallen to ground under the weight of themselves, under the weight of a grief too heavy to bear. How they become their own grief and then can no longer bear it. Whoever made this garden would have loved absolutely, whether or not that love was returned. To make these choices in the plantings required a great deal of thought and effort. For everything that was chosen, others would have been eliminated or passed over.

Someone truly loved Thomas Walton. This is the story I will make of this. Someone truly loved Thomas Walton and perhaps couldn't tell him, meant to show him with the making of this garden. Perhaps before showing this to him, the gardener cut some of the white roses and attached them to the timbered arch in my room, which was also Thomas's room.

What I can't know is if Thomas ever saw this garden. But I would say that he did. The garden had been fully planted. It was finished before the Mosel exodus to the Great War and, unless the gardener completely lost his or her nerve at the moment of unveiling, I am almost certain that Thomas would have been given this work of love. What he thought of it is impossible to guess. Was he flattered? Was he horrified? Was it like Raley and me, or was it a happier ending?

The roses look lovely in the low light, all soft and plumped up with the humidity of the morning. How could anyone turn away from that gift? No, in my story Thomas is overwhelmed with love and happiness when he is shown this garden. He will walk around it, looking at the plants and easily breaking the code of this love. He will crush the leaves of the Sweet Briar Rose between his fingers and release the scent of apples. He will understand the peonies without needing to read any descriptive label about that portion of the flower bed. He will stop before the roses. He will stop before the roses. What else is there to do?

39

I sit in the garden all day, well into evening. I am not hungry, don't make the journey back to the kitchen for food. At one point in the late afternoon I hear a car on the driveway, hear it stop outside the arch, and my first thought is that Raley has come back. But since he is the one person who would know where to find me, and he doesn't appear, I give up on that thought. I just sit there at the edge of the garden, watch it change under the shifting light of the day. When evening comes, the light leaves the ground first, moves upwards as though it's climbing out of a hole.

It is Jane who discovers me. The sun has almost gone down and the garden is murky with the early dark. There's a noise behind me in the hedge and then Jane is through the space and standing on the other side of the yews. At first I think she has come to find me, but she looks at me with such stricken surprise that I realize immediately she wasn't expecting to meet anyone here. She is wearing the sweater David was knitting those nights she read to him in the wireless room. I recognize it, and can see, even in the low, blurry light, the flecks of green in it that came from the sweater she gave him to use. This is what was in the parcel Raley delivered.

"So, this is where you're always off to," says Jane slowly, as though she's just now working it out. "I thought I was the only one who knew about this place." She comes over to me and I make room for her on the bench.

"You've been here before?" I am astonished. This is my secret place.

"Only for the past week or so. I was trimming the angel and I caught a glimpse of white over the hedge, so I slipped through and found the roses, and all those dead things." She takes out a cigarette. "Did you make it? Is it yours, Gwen?" She looks at me, her eyes dark and hollow. I have never seen her looking so bad. "Because it's exactly how I feel," she says. "It's the only thing I've found here that is exactly how I feel." She hasn't lit her cigarette yet, is plucking at the sleeve of the sweater where a thin strand of wool is starting to unravel.

Jane has discovered the garden backwards, with only the roses still in bloom. Faith to Loss to Longing. In this order it isn't a garden of love but a garden of death.

"Are you all right?" I ask.

"Did you make it?" she says again.

The light is draining from the roses. They look silver, then mauve. I can no longer see the stems connecting them to each other.

"Yes," I say. "Yes, I made it." For I have felt this afternoon that the garden does belong to me now. My story has been told here. And I am alive and the person who made the garden is most likely dead. I can look after this place, keep it tended, keep its meaning going. It is my story now.

"Come with me, then," says Jane. "I want to give you something."

There are many things I don't know yet, as we walk through the orchard to the stables, many things to come. There was a car that stopped here in the afternoon. It was the county rep, Mrs. Billings, with a letter for Jane. The letter said that they'd found the body of Andrew. He hadn't been over the ocean as expected. His plane had crashed over land. His body had been found in the woods in France, hanging from a tree by his parachute. He had been dead for months. He had been dead the entire time of his having been reported missing. He had probably only flown the first hour of his mission before being shot down. His body was badly decomposed. There was a letter from Jane in his pocket.

Jane saddles the black horse, leads him out of the stable. I don't know any of what she knows yet, but we don't speak. She helps me up onto his back, slides into the saddle in front of me, and we ride through the quadrangle, down past the walled garden, down towards the South Garden, and to the fields beyond.

These things will happen. In August, Churchill will meet Roosevelt in David's hometown of Placentia Bay, Newfoundland, and they will draft up the Atlantic Charter, unifying the war aims of the United States and Britain. At the same time Doris will go every day up the hill to the empty house the soldiers have left and she will play Ravel's "Pavane" over and over again. Sometimes I will stand outside and listen to the music as it disappears in the dusk.

The fox will take the last two chickens. I will let it happen because it has happened before, because I respect the fox's hunger and I know my need to save the chickens does not come near his need to kill them. That's what makes something seem inevitable, that imbalance of hunger and fear.

I will finally write to Virginia Woolf, a real letter, on paper. I will write about listening at the door to Jane reading *To the Lighthouse* to David while he knitted his sweaters. Dear Mrs. Woolf, I will say. Jane read your book at night, to a boy who knitted a sweater, in the middle of this war you left. And sometimes, when the wind murmurs in the trees outside my window at night it sounds like Jane reading your words aloud.

When I finish the letter I will put it in an envelope, write "Mrs. Virginia Woolf" on the front, and drop it into a letterbox. It is the only thing to do. At the time it will feel like the only thing to do.

And on the evening that I write the letter, I will go down to the wireless room, restless with purpose. At this point Jane is too weak to leave her room. Even though I have written to her parents, they arrive too late to save her. Her strict terms have been broken and her contract with the world is at an end. Before she goes, I will sit beside her bed, hold her hand, and read the names of the roses to her from *The Genus Rosa.* But before that, I go down to the wireless room and see her last act. She has finally told her story on the empty piece of blackout curtain reserved for her. Next to the others' drawings of their homes and hobbies, Jane has simply cut a large square in the fabric, made a window through which I can see the late-summer sky. I stand there for a long time before that cut-out square of cloth. And it is a beautiful day outside, this one she has given us.

Dead flowers hold their fragrance. That is one truth. Sometimes our passion is our ruin. That is another.

Jane died. Raley died. David went home. I stay on at Mosel through the war, training new groups of girls to grow potatoes, restoring the gardens of the estate, so that when the war is finally over the returning owners are so impressed with the restoration of Mosel that they offer me a position as head gardener. And I never leave. There is money again, after the war. The gardening staff is enlarged and the gardens are restored to their original splendour. The maze and the water gardens are built. Later, admission is charged to view the gardens and visitors bump about, maps in hand, viewing such oddities as the topiary angel and the old, espaliered apple trees. What isn't on the visitors' guide is the lost garden. I keep it tended, but I keep it hidden. Some people find it. Some people don't. Mostly it's children or lovers. As it should be.

Over the years a few of my gardening staff will see the ghost, for there will always be albino foxes at Mosel. Sometimes, if I am walking in the woods at night, I see again the flash of white, moving like smoke through the darkness.

Raley was killed at Dieppe in 1942, but the tree Raley and I planted continues to grow. Every spring it loses its fragrance to the earth in one reckless gesture, like a young boy standing at the railing of a ship and saying to his friend—Let us take our coats off and throw them in the sea.

David will return to Mosel, years later, with his wife and children. I will show them the estate, and then he and I will walk the grounds at dusk and he will ask me why I never left. Home is the place where we've felt the most, I will tell him. And that can be anyplace. Or anyone. It doesn't matter how long you lived there. It's what you'll always want to come back to.

I have been home twice in my life. Once when I lay under the living weight of Raley, the scent of roses beside us in the dark, and once when I rode with Jane over the fields.

Here we go, then.

My arms around her small body. The thin flame of her beating hard and clear beneath her skin. Lurch of the horse as he runs his own life down, running with that same dumb grace every night, perhaps forgetting himself and remembering himself with every stride, the way an engine spits and catches, spits and catches. Jane must be the lightest person he has ever had on his back. She must feel like no one at all, the whisper of her like the murmur of wind across his wet skin. When she stops eating and dies within two months, he will still wake at night, paw at the door of his stall, anxious for her soft weight on his back. And then, when she doesn't come and doesn't come, when the moon is full and the field ripples fluid under it like his own flanks, his own muscle pushing him across, when the horse stirs in his sleep, dreaming of running, Jane will be remembered.

I can feel Jane's breathing now, under my hands. The ratchety rise and fall of ribs. Her ribs strong and knotted like the wings of a swan. The wild flight of her heart. Too strong for breathing, it is crying. Only the feel of it riding my fingertips. The sound lost under the heavy pounding of the horse, his wet breathing.

There is a moment, when Jane either forgets or remembers that I am there, when she leans into me, lets me hold her. Her spine cleaves my chest, and, for an instant, I imagine how she would feel lying on top of me. How her bones would seem hollow. How the wind would murmur through them. Soft wind blowing in from a night window.

The thing about gardens is that everyone thinks they go on growing, that in winter they sleep and in spring they rise. But it's more that they die and return, die and return. They lose themselves. They haunt themselves.

Every story is a story about death. But perhaps, if we are lucky, our story about death is also a story about love.

And this is what I have remembered of love.

Acknowledgements

I would like to thank my agent, Frances Hanna; and my editors, Phyllis Bruce, Liz Calder, and Amy Cherry, for their care and critical acumen.

The lines from "The Wrong Road" by Richard Church are reprinted by permission of Everyman Publishers Plc.

The last four lines of "Tennessee June," used as an epigraph, are from *The Dream of the Unified Field: Poems 1974-1994* by Jorie Graham, Copyright © 1995 by Jorie Graham, reprinted by permission of HarperCollins Publishers Inc.

The newspaper reference to Virginia Woolf's disappearance is from *The Times*, April 3, 1941.

Mary Louise Adams, Elizabeth Christie, Richard Fiorino, Elizabeth Greene, Frances Humphreys, Kathy Humphreys, Shanne Humphreys, Paul Kelly, Stewart MacMillan, Daintry Norman, Joanne Page, Ruth Roach Pierson, Donna Vittorio, and Sue Worrall all provided support and assistance, literary and otherwise, during the writing of this book.

I would like to thank my father for the details of his life and his father's life that have made their way into this story.

Information and flavour about the Women's Land Army has been taken from *The Women's Land Army* by Vita Sackville-West, published under the auspices of The Ministry of Agriculture and Fisheries by Michael Joseph, London, 1944.

Details from *The Genus Rosa* have been taken from *The Genus Rosa* by Ellen Willmott, illustrations by Alfred Parsons; published by John Murray, London, 1910-14.

Details from *To the Lighthouse* are taken from *To the Lighthouse* by Virginia Woolf, first published by The Hogarth Press in 1927.

The lines from Tennyson are from "In Memoriam A.H.H.", written by Alfred Lord Tennyson from 1833-1850. The lines from the Tennyson commentary are from *Analysis of Mr. Tennyson's "in Memoriam"* by Frederick W. Robertson, Brighton, 1862.

The lines from Virgil are from Georgic IV, written in 29 B.C.E.

The information about angels is from the writings of William of Ockham (1280-1349).

For her daily words, Sue Goyette was the necessary angel during the writing of this book.

by the same author

LEAVING EARTH Helen Humphreys £6.99 0 7475 4229 5

'Extremely high-class prose. Beautifully structured ... A striking exploration of the universal need to push back boundaries' ***Observer***

It's 1933 at the height of the Great Depression and two women, Air Ace Grace O'Gorman and her young co-pilot Willa Briggs, make a bid in the skies above Toronto to break the record for non-stop flight. The current record, of 25 days in the air, is held by Grace's flight-instructor husband, Jack Robson, who is far from happy at the prospect of his wife stripping him of his title...

'Constructed with a jeweller's precision and looks back to the great age of pioneer women pilots' ***The Times***

'Humphreys' first novel is based on an actual event: her clipped, lucid prose makes the experience anything but ordinary' ***Harpers & Queen***

AFTERIMAGE Helen Humphreys £6.99 0 7475 5301 7

'Beautifully written ... leaves its own lasting, poetic image on the mind' ***The Times***

Annie arrives at a wealthy country house to work as a maid. Prepared for the grinding labour of servitude, she is startled to find herself in a world where dreams and desires are possible. Isabelle, Annie's mistress, desperately wants to become a great photographer but is thwarted by her sex and society's expectations. Using her servants as models, she creates a series of portraits of women that echo the Romantic tradition: Guinevere, Sappho, the Virgin Mary. Distanced from her husband Eldon, Isabelle finds herself irresistibly pulled into forbidden territory with Annie.

'Spectacular ... a wonderful tale of love, friendship and betrayal' ***Big Issue***

'A breath of fresh air ... Humphreys teases out a compelling tale' ***Guardian***